Thirty Phone Booths to Boston

Thirty Phone Booths

TALES OF A

to Boston WAYWARD

RUNNER

DON KARDONG

THE STEPHEN GREENE PRESS

Lexington, Massachusetts

First published in 1985 by Macmillan Publishing Company.
First published in 1987 by The Stephen Greene Press, Inc.
Distributed by Viking Penguin Inc., 40 West 23rd Street, New York, NY 10010.

This edition is reprinted by arrangement with Macmillan Publishing Company, a
division of Macmillan, Inc.

Acknowledgments appear on the following page

Library of Congress Cataloging-in-Publication Data
Kardong, Don.
Thirty phone booths to Boston.
Reprint. Originally published: New York, Macmillan, 1979.
1. Kardong, Don.   2. Runners (Sports)—United States—Biography.   I. Title. II.
Title: 30 phone booths to Boston.
GV1061.15.K37A37   1987   796.4'26   [B]   86-27105
ISBN 0-8289-0627-0

Printed in the United States of America

CONTENTS

Introduction ix

Mount St. Helens 1

The Joy of Winter 11

My Old Buick 21

Collision Course 30

Confessions of a Nutritional Agnostic 40

Dropping Out 48

Eye of the Tiger 62

1980 OLYMPIC DIARY 74

The Crab Toilet Omen 75

Elvis, Gnats, Etc. 79

President Carter's Running Mate 83

Becoming Winter 89

Money 93

The Runner Crumbles 99

Speedy Goes to the Olympics—Alone 103

Spring 1980 108

Off the Track 112

The Sunday Review 118

Thirty Phone Booths to Boston 123

Grete Waitz—New York 1980 141

Alberto Salazar, 1982 150

Fame 161

Peking, Out My Window 167

Epilogue 176

INTRODUCTION

You, there! Yes, you, standing at the back of the store, trying to decide whether to buy this book. I have a confession to make about how I moved into the writing game. Please listen.

I had nurtured, from an early age, a dream of writing something important someday, but the what, why, and when of it, in spite of English and creative writing classes, did not seem to lead anywhere in particular for quite some time. Instead, I spent most of my post-collegiate days running, training for international track and field competition. By 1974, I had become a runner of minor note, and the only writing I had done was in inventing answers to the questionnaires sent out by track and running magazines. "What is your favorite distance?" they once asked. "One light-year," I replied.

On one occasion (though I'm embarrassed to admit it), I sent a letter to *Track and Field News*, asking a silly question that I hoped would be printed. I signed the name Kelly Walters, who was my coach's son, because (does this seem too obvious?) I didn't want anyone to know the letter was from me. Kelly Walters seemed like a nondescript sort of name to use.

Kelly didn't agree. When he saw my letter printed with his name attached, he felt I had somehow scored a point in the game of life at his expense. He decided to retaliate.

Unbeknownst to me, Kelly wrote an article and sent it to *Runner's World* magazine, signing my name. I learned of his retaliation when I received a note from editor Joe Henderson, telling me that he liked my writing style but couldn't use the article.

I immediately fired off a letter to Joe, explaining that it had all been a mistake, that the article hadn't been written by me, that he shouldn't consider the deficient prose of the evil Kelly to be representative of my own, etc.

Before Joe got that letter, though, he had already written me another one.

"I really did like your writing style," he confessed, "and I understand you're going on a track and field tour to China. Would you be interested in doing an article for us?"

Thus was my writing career launched.

Today, people still refer to my style now and then, mostly in praising things I didn't write or rejecting articles I have written but which "are not the Kardong style." Is it any wonder I sometimes stare at the typewriter keys, wondering where to start?

Writer's block or not, though, this collection includes stories I've written for *Running Times*, *Running*, and *The Runner* over the past ten years. Many thanks are due to the editors of those magazines for their help, encouragement, and (generally delicate) editing.

I'm tempted to dedicate this collection to Kelly Walters, but I think I've already given him enough mention. On the other hand, "my friend Bridgid," as I refer to her in the earliest of these pieces, who has become "my wife Bridgid," since then, certainly deserves whatever honor a dedication might hold, since she put up with the rantings, ravings, mood swings, and caffeine abuse that chased most of these articles to completion. But I think I'll wait until the novel I keep promising to write is finished for that one. Now, that'll be a dedication!

This one, though, the first book, is dedicated to my parents. To my mother, who unselfishly typed the final drafts of my papers in high school while I slept soundly down the hall, and who remembered in the morning to tell me how good they were. And to my father, who still wonders what it is I do for a living. Let's hope that guy in the back buys this thing, right Dad?

And I hope he enjoys it.

Thirty Phone Booths to Boston

Mount St. Helens

SOMEHOW, someone had talked me into getting up at 6:15 on a Saturday morning. This was in many ways a more bizarre occurrence than the one that would follow. I generally use my Saturday mornings wisely, sleeping soundly as they fade into Saturday afternoons. But on this day I was up and running.

General Volney Warner, a U.S. Army four-star-studded gentleman, was in Spokane to act as grand marshal of the annual Lilac Festival Parade. He had shunned an offer of a round of golf in favor of a five-mile jaunt through one of the city parks, and I was acting as his running guide.

He and I and his aide cruised along easily, enjoying the greenery and clear air of that sunny, remarkably beautiful morning. As we ran, we talked of conditioning in general, running in particular, and of course running shoes. I noticed that the four-star general was wearing five-star shoes, a discrepancy I thought it best not to mention.

As we came to the end of the park boulevard, we turned onto another road that followed the edge of a steep embankment, where we could suddenly see miles to the southwest.

"Boy, that's beautiful," remarked the general's aide. "We don't have anything that looks like that at home."

And so we continued on our run, occasionally glancing to our left at the green hills and mist-laden valley, a picture-postcard view that in a matter of hours would be turned into an abomination of swirling gray ash.

On Sunday I made up for the previous day's early rising by sleeping until almost noon. In doing so, I'm proud to say, I slept through the greatest earthly explosion of my lifetime, louder even than the noise emitted by my father when our dog flunked her bowel and bladder control lessons for the third time back in the early sixties.

The volcanic blast of May 18, 1980, occurring some three hundred miles away, made not so much as a flatulent bark in the Spokane earscape on that day, nor had it altered the sunny weather of the previous day by so much as a candlepower by the time I got up.

I awoke to sunshine and the eerie reports of disaster on the radio.

In looking back, it seems ludicrous not to have taken more notice of impending doom. Powerful as the eruption sounded from the news reports, though, it seemed inconceivable that it would have an impact on life as far away as we were. Thus unmoved, I made plans to have breakfast with my fiancée, Bridgid, followed by an afternoon run and a flight to Missoula, Montana, for two days of physiological testing.

We had been warned over the radio that the volcanic cloud was moving our way, but as we drove along the route of Saturday's run with General Warner, the view to the southwest seemed only slightly darkened. I remembered standing on a hill east of Seattle one night in 1973, foolishly scanning the sky for any sign of Comet Kahoutek, which was promised by astronomers to be a dazzling, phenomenal streak in the heavens, but which ended up being nearly invisible. I suspected that the eruption of Mount St. Helens would turn out to be a disappointment of similar proportions.

The pancake house where Bridgid and I had breakfast was the first real catastrophe of the day. The waitress forgot to bring syrup, coffee, Coke, or silverware, and while we waited for those few items, we talked about a party we had attended the night before.

Ed, our host, had told of climbing Mount St. Helens ten or fifteen years earlier. He had stayed at the Spirit Lake Lodge, spoken with its notorious owner, Harry Truman, and enjoyed camping near the lake. As Bridgid and I were remarking on the irony of having discussed all this on the eve of the eruption, the true irony and tragedy lay in the fact that the lodge and Harry Truman himself lay, unbeknownst to anyone, under at least thirty feet of hot mud. Spirit Lake was history.

The waitress returned with silverware, forgetting syrup and cof-fee. My waffle was cold. The day was off to a bad start.

An hour later, Bridgid and I were looking out my front window at an ever-darkening sky. It was obvious by now that the passing of the volcanic cloud would be a phenomenon worthy of observation after all, but it wasn't clear exactly how dark it would get. It seemed a notion worthy of science fiction to consider the sky getting any darker than it already was.

Bridgid and I rode with my roommate Steve to the bank overlooking the Spokane River and stood gawking at the sky. It looked like an enormous cold front moving our way. Friends of mine who had failed to catch word of the eruption would later remark that that's exactly what they thought it was: an approaching storm. Strange, though, they noted, that there was no wind, coolness, or smell that accompanies such a storm.

As we watched, car headlights began to blink on and a few street lights flickered to life. We were overlooking a bridge where two weeks earlier over thirteen thousand runners had stampeded across in the 1980 Lilac Bloomsday Run. As race director, I asked myself for the first of what would be countless times during the ensuing weeks, "What if this had happened two weeks ago?"

And it continued to darken.

Back at the house, disaster reports were coming in on the radio. We heard of the enormity of the blast and of the anticipated loss of life. It finally began to sink in that this was a disaster, not just an entertaining natural phenomenon.

Still, we couldn't imagine that we would be feeling much of an impact in Spokane, and we sat entranced by the radio reports, sipping beer and enjoying the novelty of the day.

After a few minutes, the announcer began telling of the situation in Yakima, where an eighth of an inch of ash had accumulated.

"Did you hear that?" I exclaimed. "An eighth of an inch! I wonder if we'll get any?"

Bridgid suggested an experiment. She put a sheet of plain white paper on top of one of the cars, with the intention of spotting any ash that fell. *If* any fell.

A few minutes later we heard her scream, "Come see this!"

On top of the paper were a few minute dustings of ash. We were all excited. Thirty minutes later the paper was covered. We were learning quickly that the sight of ash was nothing to get excited about.

Meanwhile, it had become almost pitch black. In the headlights of cars leaving a nearby golf course we could see swirling clouds of volcanic dust. It looked like a very cold, powdery snowfall in the dark. Cars were being covered with it, as well as trees and houses. As well as everything. It looked unhealthy.

A girl came riding down the street on her bicycle, and Steve yelled at her, "Hey, get out of this stuff!"

"What is this, anyway?" she yelled back.

"It's ash from a volcanic eruption," he shouted.

There was a slight pause as she rode away, followed by a cynical, just barely audible, "Yeah, sure."

We went back inside and listened to the radio in the dark. People were dead, cars were stranded, flights were grounded. It began to feel like disaster. I got up, walked to the refrigerator, and popped another beer.

By this time the airport was closed down, meaning, of course, that I had no way of reaching Missoula. For a variety of inane reasons, this was the fourth time I had been unable to get there as scheduled, and I would have been embarassed to cancel again without the ironclad excuse at my disposal. I dialed Ned Frederick, who was planning to meet me at the airport.

"Ned, this is Don."

"Don?" There was a slight, what-is-it-this-time pause. "What's going on?"

"Ned, I know this is going to sound like another one of my excuses, but I can't get over there because of a volcanic eruption."

After my earnest explanation, Ned politely refused to believe me. The hour of ashfall in Missoula had not yet arrived. I stuck to my bizarre story, though, until he reluctantly pretended to believe it. We agreed to reschedule for another time.

Having freed up my afternoon by canceling the Missoula trip, and having stared out the window for a long time as the sky lightened and revealed a landscape powdered with gray, nasty-looking ash that choked the air and threatened to destroy the lungs of anyone who ventured outside, and having downed my third Oly, there remained only one possible course of action for the afternoon. I turned to Steve.

"Let's go. We've got to run in this."

In ten minutes, clad in shorts, T-shirts, handkerchiefs, dark glasses, and absurdity, we were off and running.

The ash was still falling, and without dark glasses the tiny bits of pumice seemed to burn the eyes. The handkerchiefs, moistened and worn over nose and mouth, gave the impression of protection for our lungs. The overall visual effect was bizarre. Butch Cassidy and the Some Dunce Kid.

We ran three miles, long enough to realize we didn't want to be out there at all, let alone out there running. (A friend of mine asked later if we looked "ashen and pale," a la Jimmy Carter, when we returned.)

Our run had not gone unnoticed, as we discovered later in the day, when we ran to the grocery story for food and more beer. The girl there recognized us as "the joggers" she had seen earlier. She refused to help us, or even look at us, muttering "Idiots" every time we walked by.

Back home, we settled down for dinner and what appeared to be a long siege. On the radio we heard that schools and businesses would be closed the next day. Later, the announcer let us know that a second cloud from the eruption had reached Yakima, would reach Spokane after midnight, and was expected to darken the sky again. "Of course it'll already be dark then, though," he said, and then added awkwardly, "So . . . we won't notice it."

By this time, though, sunshine at midnight wouldn't have seemed unusual.

Having grown up as I did in Seattle, where snow is as unusual as sunshine, I remember the feeling of waking after a freak snowstorm and hearing school cancellations on the radio. That's what Monday morning after the eruption felt like.

The snow analogy seemed appropriate in other ways, too. Spokanites, used to dealing patiently with accumulations of white stuff in the winter, were using similar methods to deal with the quarter inch of ash that covered everything. Snow shovels were blazing and brooms were flailing in an attempt to impose order on the chaotic landscape.

People were beginning to wash down streets, yards, houses, and trees with garden hoses, though the question of whether a combination of ash and water would produce sulfuric acid was unanswered, and the problem of what the tons of ash being washed into the sewage system would do was also unsolved.

Other questions—Will there be more ashfall? Should masks be moist or dry? Will our drinking water be poisoned? How long will this last?—continued to mystify all of us. With the vague smell of sulfur and ash in the air, with the absence of auto traffic producing surrealistic, stifling stillness, and with the health questions associated with breathing ash unanswered, I decided not to run that day.

Airport closed. Exercise dangerous. In one week the U.S. Olympic Marathon Trials would take place in Buffalo. I was glad, for the first time, that the Olympic boycott had cancelled my interest in that race. It would have been unsettling, to say the least, trying to deal with the eruption if a major race were only a few days away at the other end of the country.

Tuesday brought few answers to the many bizarre questions people were asking about volcanic dust, but it did bring irony to the surface for those who appreciate such things.

This was the first day that, walking to the grocery store, I noticed someone wearing an unusual mask. I was prompted to respond as one might in admiring a new shirt: "Hey, what an interesting mask. Where'd you get it?" Somehow I managed to avoid speaking those silly lines, although it did seem that everyone's interest in ash-masks as apparel was growing.

In the ensuing weeks the discussions raged back and forth about which masks to wear, whether to moisten them or not, and how effective they actually were.

No one really had any concrete evidence as to whether breathing the ash was dangerous. After a while people began to speak of "silicosis," a lung disease common to coal miners, and a few respiratory pundits dragged "pneumonoultramicroscopicsilicovolcanoconiosis" out of the bottom drawer and began waving it around.

Once again irony. In seventh or eighth grade a friend of mine had brought the word to school one day, thus supplanting "antidisestablishmentarianism" as the lengthiest word anyone knew. I had carried pneumonoultramicroscopicsilicovolcanoconiosis around in my mind for almost twenty years, occasionally rolling it around my tongue, enjoying its comical scientific rhythms, having no idea what it meant. Now, possibly, I was dying of it.

Most people were taking no chances with volcanic ash, especially since it was suggested that it might be carcinogenic. Masks of every shape and form appeared in an effort to combat the possible cancerfiend. The irony this time was in seeing people who smoked cigarettes suddenly worried about lung disease.

In the weeks ahead, people were spotted who had pushed their ash-masks up on their foreheads so they could enjoy a smoke. At least one clever inventor showed up in public wearing a mask in which a small hole had been cut to allow a cigarette to be inserted.

Irony also lay in the fact that this was the second day of Spokane's "Non-Polluter Commuter Week," a brand-new civic celebration to encourage alternative transportation. I talked with one of the organizers of the event a few days later and told her she had done an excellent job of reducing automobile traffic, though I hadn't noticed a great improvement in air quality as a result.

The ironies of Tuesday, coupled with the numerous unanswered questions and a good dose of cabin fever, led me to begin running again. I donned moistened handkerchief and headed down toward the river on a nine-miler.

Running that day was like training on the inside of a vacuum-cleaner bag or the bottom of an ashtray. The lighter part of the ashfall easily blew in the air, making breathing uncomfortable in spite of the mask.

I stopped occasionally during my run to observe tracks in the ash: Birds' and mammals' were easily spotted, but most amazing of all were the insect tracks. So fine was the volcanic powder that insects as small as mosquitoes made observable tracks as they struggled to get airborne.

Bees, laden with dust rather than pollen, fell to the ground and struggled to free themselves of the fine powder. It was possible to follow their paths of death in the ash, marks that looked like the tire tracks of tiny unicycles, circling awkwardly around and around and finally crashing. I never expect, no matter how long I live, to observe the death-tracks of bees again.

My run ended with two miles through city neighborhoods, where the scene of masked people hosing down their property and nearby streets was one of postnuclear catastrophe. I know the sight of a runner must have provoked curiosity, amusement, and even anger among the infrequent passing motorists, but with the dust flying no one seemed to care about rolling down windows to shout insults.

I returned home tired, and especially tired of battling a Mother Nature who seemed to have been so frivolous with her ill favors.

Wednesday marked the third day that my store, The Human Race, had been closed. During a morning run, I sensed that the worst part of the disaster was over, since only the passage of cars and the dust clouds they raised made running uncomfortable. Otherwise, it was tolerable, and it seemed that an attempt at going back to work was in order. Perhaps the next day.

I got a telephone call a little later. "Is this the last surviving member of the Human Race?" It was my partner Rick.

We decided to open the store the next morning, though it seemed unlikely that people in town would be chomping at the bit to buy new running shoes. We were very likely going to face severe problems as a result of the sudden loss of income, and we talked of ways we might try to turn the disaster around by selling souvenir T-shirts ("I survived the Mount St. Helens Summit Run: May 18, 1980") or having a special Get-Off-Your-Ash-and-Run sale.

"After all," I told him, "if you can't make money off a disaster, you're not a true American."

"Well, all I can say," he replied, "is that none of this would have happened if Portland had had their annual procession of virgins this year to appease the volcano."

"Why didn't they have it this year?" I asked, the eternal straight man.

"One of them was sick," he answered, "and the other one didn't want to march alone."

I spent the rest of the day in the yard, hosing down the roof, trees, and cars. The assault by the volcanic enemy had created a bond among neighbors as everyone struggled for the third straight day to clean up the mess. I felt the sense of community that must have prevailed during World War II, when people shared a common enemy.

The desire for a return to normalcy was very strong, but no one seemed to know when normalcy might be expected to show its face again. How long would life be dusty?

The evening news spoke of riots in Miami and the human disaster at the Love Canal near Niagara Falls, as well as the fact that President Carter would be flying out west to observe our volcanic problems. Hearing of Niagara Falls reminded me of the forthcoming Olympic Marathon Trials, and once again I speculated on what my thoughts and emotions might have been if that race had remained a priority for me. I hadn't heard an airplane flying overhead since the eruption, and most of the highways were still closed. It would have been one hell of a struggle to get out of town.

The local news showed more pictures of disaster and continued to give contradictory information on what the long-term effects of the ash might be. "What we really need," said one newscaster, "is a good rainfall." She turned to the weatherman. "Is there any rain in the forecast?"

"I wish I could say that there was," he replied. He went on to describe the dry, dusty conditions our area could expect for the foreseeable future.

I watched television a little longer, then picked up a book I had nearly finished, *The Collector* by John Fowles. The story of a woman imprisoned in a psychopath's basement and her yearning for fresh air had a peculiar resonance by this time. How long would we have to wait for a rainfall to wash this stuff away, so that all of us could breathe fresh air again?

Then I heard it. Or maybe I just sensed a change. I went to the front door and opened it, and a breeze of hope blew in. It was raining!

In a few minutes the sky that had promised no precipitation was dumping enormous bucketsful, washing the ash out of trees, off houses, down sewers, into the river.

The rain would continue through the night, and though the morning would be fresh, the ash would fly again and again, resisting like an unwelcome visitor any attempt to send it on its way.

In the ensuing weeks, the rains would continue periodically with unusual vigor, as if Mother Nature were trying to atone for her volcanic wrongdoing. It would be almost a month before people stopped worrying about pneumonoultramicroscopicsilicovolcano-coniosis and began breathing easy. There would be many more dusty days, some incredibly bad ones, and innumerable discussions on potential health problems.

The effects of the eruption on Spokane would continue for weeks, months, even years, and yet standing there in the doorway as the rain fell, I realized with relief that nature was already beginning the long process of renewal. The next day, Thursday, I would run ten miles without a mask.

The Joy of Winter

I BEGAN my running career in Seattle, though that fact only muddies the issue. I began running, I think, in spite of Seattle. Or at least in spite of its weather. It doesn't rain a lot in Seattle, so the saying goes, it just rains all the time.

I once heard a disc jockey in Spokane reading what he claimed was a letter from his mother in Seattle. "It's been beautiful weather here this past week," his mother wrote. "It's only rained twice. Once for two days, once for four."

And how about the Seattle method of weather prognostication: If you can see Mt. Rainier, it's going to rain. If you can't, it's already raining.

And on and on. Seattlites hate this kind of talk. To them, Perry Como said it right: "The bluest skies you've ever seen are in Seattle." I prefer it my own way: "The bluest skies you've never seen are in Seattle."

I hate this weather. I detest running in it.

The progression of my athletic career in this climate was logical up to its final point. I gave up baseball, a career destined to be rained out anyway, after I missed the practice where uniforms were handed out, and ended up with a uniform that made me look like a stick in a garbage bag. I forsook football after choosing to be a tackle (that's another story), and suffering rain-soaked on the sidelines through my first game. I abandoned golf after losing yet another ball in the middle of a muddy fairway. I thought it was unfair that a ball hit straight toward the green, perhaps a trifle high, should be allowed to disappear upon impact with a swampy fairway. Archaeologists may wonder about this some day.

And so, logically, I played basketball, an indoor sport. And there it should have ended.

"What are you doing to get ready for basketball?" the coach asked me one day.

"I don't know," I answered. "Shooting a few baskets now and then. What should I do?"

"Why don't you run cross-country?"

Looking back on it, I suspect he was looking for a way to get rid of me. Really, does cross-country help basketball? Does Dr. J jog? Anyway, before I knew what had happened I was a long-distance runner, with soggy gray sweats that weighed thirty pounds and socks around my ankles. I was all wet.

At the time, the rain really didn't bother me. I had grown up in that climate. I had built models of the greatest hydroelectric projects in the world in ditches near my house, until the police told me I was eroding the roadbed. I had gone camping with the Boy Scouts in that weather, huddling in tents while the rain drummed happily on the canvas top, until I read in the manual that moss grows on the north side of a tree. In the Northwest, it grows all the way around, which caused me much confusion and disillusionment with Boy Scout wisdom. I had lived in that weather for years without even knowing my hair was wet. Then I graduated from high school and headed south.,

One would assume this was the subconscious speaking, making some kind of urge of its own felt. If I hadn't realized it yet, my subconscious seemed to know that I hated this cold, miserable wetness. Running in California would be wonderful, just what I needed. Wouldn't it?

When I left, my mother gave me an umbrella as a gift, the first I had ever owned. Though she seemed guileless, I suspect she knew something I didn't. Who ever heard of taking an umbrella to California?

At this point you may think I'm going to tell you a story about how it rains in California. You think I'm going to tell a story like this one:

On the way to the Honolulu Marathon last December, I stopped in San Francisco and gave fellow runner Roy Kissin a call. We made arrangements to go for a long run on Mount Tamalpais, in spite of the chance of continued rainfall.

"Once we get in under the trees we'll be pretty well protected," Roy said, believing it.

"Roy," I asked him as we began our run, "what's the worst you've ever been deceived on a run?"

"What do you mean?"

"Well, you know. Someone tells you a run is five miles and it ends up ten. Or they say it's flat and it's really hilly. That kind of thing."

"I don't know," he said after a pause. "What's yours?"

I realized I didn't have a good answer. "I don't know either," I said, surprised. "I wonder what made me think of the question."

As we headed up the road into the park, Roy looked at the gray sky. "It looks like it's letting up," he said. "We might have timed this perfectly." Meanwhile, as we entered the "shelter" of the trees, huge drops of water began falling from the leaves above us.

"What's your misery quotient?" Roy asked, as the wetness began to soak through.

"My misery quotient?"

"Yeah, you know. One-to-ten. Mine's about a five."

"I'd have to go with a five, too," I said. "As long as I'm warm I'm all right."

We continued running up the mountain along a muddy trail for another twenty minutes, and as we rounded one turn the wind hit us full force. "Roy," I yelled, "I'm a six."

"Don't worry," he yelled back. "I'm a six too, but we'll be out of the wind and onto a level section at the top of this hill."

"Which hill?" I screamed. "The one we've been on for the last forty-five minutes?"

"Yeah, that one," he said, grinning soggily. "Mount Tam."

We did finally crest the hill and get out of the wind, but the rain was increasing, and my misery quotient edged up another point.

"I'm a seven, Roy, and the only thing that keeps me from being an eight is the scenery here. It's beautiful."

"It's even better when you can see it," he said.

We hadn't seen anyone else along the way, but as we ran around one of the reservoirs we spotted a crew of workmen in yellow slickers burning dead wood. They seemed more interested in staying close to the fire than collecting wood, and as we passed on the trail near them they all stopped to stare at the sight of two thinly clad runners moving through the woods. Interesting comments must have passed between them regarding our presence there.

A mile or two later we passed the furthest point in our voyage and turned to head home. We ran out of the woods and across the top of one of the dams, and this time we were hit in the face by a forty-mile-an-hour wind and near-freezing rain. The hood of my rain jacket was flapping against my ears like a canvas truck-bed covering on the freeway, and I struggled to keep Roy in sight ahead of me as we followed the narrow path around the reservoir. The wind was gusting hard enough to blow whichever leg was off the ground out of its normal stride, and at one point my legs got tangled up and I fell. Roy, unaware of the fall, kept running. An image of him getting most of the way back to the car before realizing I wasn't behind him came to mind. I struggled to my feet and ran to catch up.

"Roy!" I screamed, so he could hear me through the storm. "I'm a full-blown ten!"

"Right!" he yelled back.

The misery quotient of ten lasted only a few minutes, until we managed to get back among the trees. The thought that we were on our way back down the mountain, and that we would soon be finished with this madness, brought it back to a more respectable level.

"I think I lied back there," I told him. "It was only a nine-and-a-half."

"That's all right," he said. "I understand."

"You want to know something, though," I said.

"What's that?"

"I've finally figured out the worst I've ever been deceived on a run."

I didn't mean to tell that story. I was talking about the rain I grew up with in Seattle, and I was talking about moving to California with my new umbrella, and the implication is that it was the same thing all over again. Such was not the case.

Certainly I remember rain in the Bay Area, running intervals in the tunnels of Stanford stadium to avoid the downpour, listening to the complaints of native Texans on the team about the bad weather; but I also have trouble thinking of more than a handful of times during college when rain upset our workouts. But I finally figured out why my mother gave me an umbrella, even though I'm sure she didn't realize it.

It was because there was no variety in California weather, just as there was no variety in the weather I grew up with. It was the same problem in a different guise. In Seattle it was gray, with "the bluest skies you've ever seen" every other February 29th, and in California it was the other way around. Neither way was healthy, and when I finally realized that, I moved to Spokane.

In Spokane, and throughout the vast breadbasket of the nation that does not live in either perpetual rain or perpetual shine, there exists something called winter, something that I saw pictures of when I was growing up. Currier and Ives kind of thing, an image of Christmas on the farm, with snow on the ground and smoke out the chimney and grandma and grandpa at the door. I was nostalgic for winter before I had ever experienced one, and I remain to this day convinced of the value of winter in the overall scheme of things.

In an area with four seasons, life is always getting better. Take running, for example.

Spring running is better than winter running because it's easier to stay warm and the streets aren't icy. Summer running is better than spring because it doesn't rain and you can get a tan while you run. Fall running is better than summer because you don't have to worry about getting heatstroke and the scenery is gorgeous. Winter running is better than fall because you can relax from competition and get your aching body back together.

How hard is it to convince yourself that no matter how bad running is at any particular time, in a month or two it'll be better?

And aside from that argument, there are those who will actually maintain that of all periods of the year, their favorite time for running is in deep dark dreadful winter. Why?

Because in the dead of winter life is not dead, it's dormant. Goals have a way of reshaping themselves in anticipation of spring. Competitive plans simmer. In the frozen expectations of dark winter running, dreams are conceived. Warm clouds of breath puff into chilled air, long-johned legs work rhythmically, a lone runner hears the squeak of waffle soles as he propels himself along a snow-crusted, tree-shadowed, star-lit road.

"How would you know? You're never here in the winter," says Bridgid, my wife.

"What do you mean, I'm never here?" I return.

"You're in Hawaii, or Florida, or Bermuda, or . . ."

"I'm here for most of it. I love running in the winter."

"Anyone with a tan line where you have a tan line shouldn't be talking about winter running."

"What tan line?"

"You know where it is. . . ." End of discussion.

Nevertheless, I do love running in the winter. I feel strength developing. I feel dreams flourishing. I feel confidence building. I feel that the struggle of maintaining a training program at freezing temperatures improves my will power.

Think of all the great runners who have come from frozen winter wastelands in the Midwest and Northeast: Lindsay, Meyer, Rodgers, Virgin. Isn't this cause for thought?

"They all go to Hawaii and Florida too," Bridgid reminds me.

"Yes, but they didn't used to," I reply. I thought this discussion was over. "Winter running is what makes them tough. It tempers the spirit."

Bridgid rolls her eys. "Why do you leave all the time, then?"

No answer.

I once asked Garry Bjorklund if it was true that runners from Minneapolis, as I had heard, ride the bus ten miles into the wind on a cold day so that they can run home with a tailwind.

"I've never done that," he responded. "It does get cold there, though. I once ran when the air temperature was minus forty and the wind was blowing. The chill factor made it a hundred below."

He told me this during a training run in Hawaii.

It isn't easy, by the way, to get to Hawaii, Florida, and Bermuda. You have to go through Chicago or Newark or Washington, D.C. I ran once across the Mall in D.C. when the wind was whirling enormous clouds of snow all around me. The only humans outside gritted their teeth, squinted their eyes, covered their ears, and dreamed of the Bahamas as they followed the single line of runners ahead of them, like prospectors climbing a narrow mountain pass into the Yukon, nurturing strange dreams of success. Runners.

The next day I was in Florida.

I ran once, when I saw nowhere close to my hotel where a runner might reasonably be expected to train, through an area of New Jersey where young kids gathered around burning trash barrels for warmth and women in fishnet stockings yelled, "Hey, nice legs, honey," from inside the fur coats where they huddled as I passed.

The next day I was in Bermuda.

I ran once in Spokane when there was no wind, only the chilly temperature and the still whiteness of a winter evening, lit by a full moon. Nice.

The next day I was in Winnipeg. After all, I don't always get to fly south for the winter.

Perhaps if winter weren't dark as well as cold, more runners would appreciate the season. But something about the invention of daylight savings time, and the way all the summer light we become accustomed to suddenly disappears when every clock in the country falls back an hour, makes the onset of winter a catastrophic rather than gradual event. We are suddenly running blind as well as cold. I like this too.

Perhaps I enjoy winter running on account of the darkness more than the cold. I have always resonated spiritually to the image of distance running as a solitary sport, a personal journey, a monastic pursuit. Nothing fulfills this image more than an evening winter run. The self-defined hero battling the elements and dreaming of

victory in the spring, striding quietly through the faint fading-orange
February dusk.

"Would you hurry up and run if you're going to run," Bridgid
tells me as I dawdle in front of the TV, dressed in long underwear,
mittens, and sweatshirt, gulping coffee.

"I have to wait for my caffeine buzz," I tell her. "It's cold out
there, you know. And it's dark. I need this unsettling caffeine nudge
to get out the door."

"Well, hurry up and get it over with."

And finally out the door I go, enlivened by the coffee, more
attuned to the mellow symphonies Mother Nature will provide during the run. The coffee has heightened my perceptions. Plus, I can't
sit still.

I was conceived, as I once determined, under the influence of a
full moon. I was born on the shortest day of the year. Is it any
wonder I have this affinity for running in the dark?

Magical things happen during a dark run. An undetermined
animal, high up in a tree, screeches as I pass. A shooting star drops
toward the horizon. An owl asks, "Whoooo?" A lone bird floats in
front of the moon. The river passes in shards of reflected light. I
hear movement in the bushes.

This is the stuff of dreams, unfolding.

I strode easily around a city park one December evening, the
fog thickly settled in the trees around me, an uneasy stillness sitting
with it. In the midst of the city, I felt alone as I ran. Suddenly I
was aware of music, coming from one of the side streets. Christmas
music. As it got louder I noticed a glow coming from the same
direction, and I realized that an apparition was materializing out of
the mist. In a few seconds I recognized Santa Claus and his reindeer,
passing through the streets of the city to the tunes of the season.
Santa Claus, visiting me during my run!

"That was a Santa Claus float," Bridgid told me later. "The
shopping center hires someone to drive it around to drum up business."

"It was nice, though," I told her. The next time I saw Santa in
the store I winked. He winked back.

How can one compare this kind of winter epiphany, with all its promises and satisfactions, to the groveling in the rain and flirting with heatstroke that is running in other seasons and other locations? Winter running is its own reward.

"Then why do you leave?" Bridgid would ask.

Good question, of course. Why? Because the glitter wears off when the temperature hits twenty below. Because the glamour wears thin when you twist your ankle for the third time in a week or you trip and become a human snowball on the pavement. Because the glory wears ragged when your breath has frozen in tiny ice-balls in your moustache, beard, and sideburns, and your nose is beginning to twitch in the first throes of frostbite.

That's when, if I can't fly south, I head for an indoor track.

Indoor running isn't so much an alternative to winter running as it is a respite, a pause, and a jewel with its own facets. Winter runners like myself learn to appreciate the weekly experience of driving to the nearest facility, changing into shorts and T-shirts, and dropping into the rhythm of an interval workout while the snow falls outside.

There is even the special satisfaction of dodging the tennis players, baseball jocks, and fitness joggers as we tear around the turns at breakneck pace.

"Get out of the way!" someone yells in encouragement.

"Out of the first two lanes!" screams a tennis player.

"Track! Track! Track!" we shout in response.

How can you beat this kind of enjoyment?

And the end of this weekly ceremony, the icing on the cake, is to visit the local grocery store, buy beer and munchies, and take our time driving back to town. Earl plays "In-A-Gadda-Da-Vida" on the tape deck while we drive the back road, recalling our lap times and watching our driver maneuver the icy road ahead. We may even stop at the downtown YMCA for a whirlpool and enjoy a few minutes of hot-tub satisfaction and the unusual joy of seeing bikinis in midwinter as the snow falls outside.

It is a long time from that first chilly autumn day when you realize you're running your morning run clad only in shorts and

T-shirt while the reader board flashes thirty-five degrees as you pass, to the day in March when you finally sense that winter's chokehold on Mother Nature is beginning to relax and you can begin looking for the first signs of spring.

But it finally does happen. You realize that it's been getting lighter every evening and that you're beginning to see where you're stepping as you run.

You sense rebirth in the woods. The ground is moist from melted snow and soft under your feet as you run over it. You imagine the yellow bursts of wild daisies that will punctuate the forest floor in a few weeks. You smell pine in the air. A squirrel squeaks and scurries as you pass. And you realize that somehow all the wonder of this recurring cycle has earned its poignancy as counterpoint to innumerable dark, frozen runs along the same route. Runs that are fading in memory, melting under the onslaught of spring.

Nevertheless, there are a lot of evenings when the peculiar rewards of a tooth-gritting, frozen-cheeked, finger-numbing, frigid-muscled run are not immediately apparent. One January evening at a local restaurant I eavesdropped on a conversation at the table behind me.

"You know what was great about being in Seattle this week?" I heard a man say. "I could run without bundling up and freezing my lungs. I could actually run without having my feet slip out from under me. It was enjoyable to run again."

"Didn't it rain?" someone asked.

"Yeah, but who cares?"

I restrained myself with great effort, while outside the snow continued to fall.

My Old Buick

I HAD GONE through ten miles of the Twin Cities Marathon in fifty-two minutes. Nothing spectacular, but nothing to be ashamed of. A final time in the 2:16 range seemed likely.

A minute later, I was hunched over at the side of the road, hands on my knees, stomach churning, and speaking to Ralph, as we used to say. I was thinking about my old Buick.

The Buick, a powder-blue Skylark that carried me through high school and college in admirable fashion, was zipping through Northern California one day in 1971 on its way back to Washington, with myself and fellow runner Duncan Macdonald inside, when it began lurching in syncopated fashion. We pulled off the highway, opened the hood, and looked at an engine that had suffered some sort of losing bout with the heat. Water from the radiator had sprayed the underside of the hood and was dripping from the water pump.

We waited for things to cool down a little, then took the next freeway exit to a service station.

"I'm sure it's the thermostat," said the attendant. "Those things clog up in the winter and get stuck when they're supposed to open."

He replaced it, we drove happily down the highway, and twenty minutes later the engine overheated again. We found another station.

"I'd guess it's the thermostat," the attendant said.

"We just replaced it," I told him.

"Well, sometimes even the new ones stick. I can replace it if you want."

He did, and we headed off again. We overheated, found another service station, and heard a familiar story.

"Probably the thermostat," the man said.

"We've replaced the thermostat twice," I said.

"Well," he replied, "maybe you should just take it out. That way the coolant will be sure to circulate."

We left, drove, overheated, found another station.

"Probably the thermostat," the man said.

"I've replaced it twice and finally took it out altogether," I said, overheating myself. "There isn't even one in there."

"Not one in there?" he said, surprised. "No wonder you're having trouble. You've got to have a thermostat." He put one in.

Twenty-four hours and a few futile, costly repairs later, we deserted the car and caught a bus to Washington.

And now, a dozen years later in Minneapolis, with my hands on my knees and my stomach in revolt, I was remembering the feelings of frustration I had faced in trying to get that old car going again. Sometimes, it seems, no matter who you consult or what you do, the same old problem keeps rising to the surface, bobbing and weaving in an elusive attempt to avoid getting fixed. And in running the marathon, whatever slight maladjustment might be in one's system is bound to become a major obstacle to success. The old Buick had finally succumbed to a flaw, not unlike the one that hit me at the ten-mile mark in Minneapolis. The Buick's flaw was in the gurgling innards of its system. So was my own.

The first time I remember experiencing midrace nausea was during the 1976 Baltimore Marathon. At the prerace pasta feed, local runner Marge Rosasco asked whether I had ever had trouble with my stomach during a race.

"I used to have trouble with a side stitch," I told her. "Two-thirds of the way into a five- or ten-K race I'd get a really sharp pain in my side. One of the reasons I switched to running marathons was because I don't have the problem in the longer race."

"How about nausea, though?" she asked. "I keep running marathons where I get to about twenty miles feeling fine, right on the pace I want, when all of a sudden I get sick to my stomach. I've tried all sorts of things to cure it, but nothing seems to work. Have you ever had anything like that?"

I was no help to her. The problem with the side stitch had been a recurrent one in college, especially on cross-country courses. I had altered my diet, adjusted my breathing, strengthened my stomach muscles, and tried taking medication to prevent spasm of the colon.

Nothing really helped much, though, except moving on to another event.

But throwing up during a race?

"I haven't had that problem since high school, Marge, when I was totally out of shape."

The next day I spent ten minutes next to the road at the nineteen-mile mark, stomach heaving uncontrollably, eyes bulging, knees shaking.

"There must be something in the water in this part of the country," I told Marge later.

An old car may perform beautifully for years, dutifully chauffeuring its owner from place to place, never showing great signs of distress, only to suffer a major breakdown when asked to push to the limit on the open road. Runners are not much different, which is why the marathon tends to bring out the worst in us.

Not everyone suffers from midmarathon nausea, but it does seem that most of us have some sort of frailty that peeks its problematic head up during the excessive stresses of the marathon race, or at least during marathon training. At the Twin Cities Marathon the second-fastest American of all time, Dick Beardsley, was suffering through a prolonged absence from his specialty and was working on TV coverage of the race instead. Beardsley's achilles heel has been his achilles tendon, and an operation to correct the problem had sidelined him for months.

"The doctor told me I could be running up to ten miles a day by November," he said.

I didn't tell him about the thermostats.

In fact, injuries incurred during training and racing are much more common than sensitive stomachs in interfering with people's marathon attempts. Many runners find that the amount of training necessary to allow them to feel comfortable running the marathon is well beyond the amount they can handle without sustaining an injury. Usually it's a knee, a hip, an arch, or, as in Beardsley's case, a bad tendon or two that become wrenches in the marathon machinery. And the exact cure is often elusive.

For years I suffered from a sharp pain in my left knee, which was especially acute during downhill running. After five or six years of flirting with ice, aspirin, and cortisone treatments, the pain finally subsided with the development of better running shoes. Apparently the problem was bursitis, but knowing that didn't seem to help much. And though doctors in recent years have gotten better at treating the well-hidden glitches in human athletic machinery, they're not always sympathetic to the excesses of long-distance runners.

A college teammate of mine who had injured his knee complained to his doctor that the joint would tighten up when he tried to run more than five miles a day.

The doctor was incredulous. "Well then, don't *run* more than five miles a day," he said.

It made sense, of course, unless one was tempted by longer distances. And when we pursue faster times at the marathon distance, we generally end up asking doctors to cure things that most people have sense enough to treat by avoiding the cause. Fatal athletic flaws tend to lie outside the realm of ordinary medicine, and as a result we runners often end up speculating about the root of the problem ourselves.

After my first bout with nausea at Baltimore, I was convinced that the only problem had been in the city's water supply. The next year I decided to run in Hawaii. By then, I had forgotten about the nausea.

On the night before the race, Duncan Macdonald and I went out for Mexican food. The next day, I wound up with my hands on my knees at nineteen miles, and Duncan won the race. I suspected foul play.

It seemed reasonable, though, given my own penchant for enjoying an outrageous diet, and given the delicious complexity of our meal the night before, that something in the Mexican dinner was at fault. If not, perhaps the aid stations were to blame.

Thus began the dietary phase of my problem solving, when I adjusted everything on the menu to avoid stomach complications during the race. I passed up electrolyte fluids at the aid stations, then stopped drinking anything at all. I avoided excessive carbohydrate loading the night before the race and stayed away from spicy foods. The next year I won the Honolulu Marathon. My problem, it seemed, had been solved.

Remember the Buick, though? We had deserted it in Northern California, frustrated to the hilt with trying to fix it. But after a week or two, I had it loaded on a truck and shipped home. A local mechanic installed a new engine, and everything seemed to work fine.

"It still runs a little hot," he confided. "But I don't think you'll have a problem with it."

I had my doubts. After repeated service-station stops along the highway in California, my confidence in fixing flaws was not high. I drove slowly in the cool of the night when I headed back to California in the fall. In spite of my caution, the car showed signs of overheating. Before long, I was aware that it wasn't truly fixed and that I would have to avoid long, hot drives if I didn't want a recurrence of the problem.

My marathon "solution," careful attention to prerace and midrace diet, worked out better for a while. I ran several races without hearing much from my stomach. In its place, other problems, mostly muscular, cropped up.

During my two successive Boston Marathons, I developed severe tightness in my calves from the early downhill running, and I realized that a tall runner was destined to have trouble on the Boston course. The second year I proved it to myself by cramping acutely and dropping out at the sixteen-mile point.

It may be that muscular quirks are the fatal flaws of marathon runners more than all other weaknesses put together. Could there be more convincing evidence of the impropriety of human beings racing the marathon distance than the fact that our muscles tend to run out of glycogen at twenty miles? Even I wouldn't expect my Buick to continue down the highway without stopping to fill up every now and then. But I do seem to expect my body to continue running indefinitely on empty.

I'm not sure how many marathons I've run where I've "hit the wall," the phrase we all use to describe muscular despair during the latter stages of the race. But I remember two in a row that, in retrospect, seem typical. The first was in the fall of 1980, when I dodged traffic in the tunnels of Rio de Janeiro for thirty kilometers before slowing precipitously for the final 5K along the beach. With blisters ("the size of Buicks," Woody Allen would say) on both feet, I was told by a spectator that all I had to do was keep moving and I'd get third. I kept moving and finished sixth.

The second, a few months later in Japan, saw me standing at an aid station just past twenty miles, pouring down one cup of juice after another, desperately trying to restore my blood sugar level. After my third cup, the spectators began to chuckle. Embarrassed, I hobbled off toward the finish line.

A friend of mine was once in a similar wasted condition in the last few miles of a marathon, and he convinced himself that he was making progress down the road by sighting objects up ahead, then monitoring his progress toward them. At one point he spotted a pedestrian several hundred yards ahead and made that person his immediate goal.

Staring down at his feet, he ran for a while, then looked up. Not much progress. He looked down at his feet again, ran some more, looked up again. Unbelievably, he still didn't seem to have gotten much closer. Was it possible someone was walking faster than *he* was running? Finally, after concentrating on his feet and running as long as he could before looking up, he recognized some progress toward his goal. And as he got closer, he suddenly realized that the pedestrian had been walking *toward* him the whole time.

Muscular fatigue, cramping, and depletion, though, no matter how drastic, are just part of the game. Proper training and adjustments in the diet can help alleviate these flaws in our makeup, but can the same be said of regurgitation?

To correct my problems with muscular exhaustion, I went into my next marathon after a full program of carbohydrate depletion and loading. I felt confident of having stored plenty of glycogen for the final miles of the race, convinced that I wouldn't be frustrated by a lack of energy. I was right. Instead, I threw up again.

This time, a woman runner and physiologist I talked to suggested that the nausea was actually a symptom of heatstroke. I had suffered from the heat in Rio de Janeiro, she said, and when you've been knocked down by the heat, it can throw the system off for months and months. The body's ability to regulate its temperature is thrown off, sort of like having a problem with . . . a thermostat.

Well, why not? The cure, then, was to avoid marathons for a while, let the body reestablish its ability to control its own internal heat. This was fine with me. I was planning to give up the event altogether.

For a year and a half I passed up all opportunities to run the twenty-six-miler. The rest did me good, I'm sure; but the attractions of the marathon are many, and by the fall of 1982 I was back in serious training. After months of preparation, I jumped back into the fray at Honolulu. I suffered some nausea at the twenty-one-mile aid station, but the results weren't drastic. I finished ninth, and vowed to try another. In January, I ran 2:16:41 at Houston. Some nausea again, but only briefly. My confidence was returning. For my third marathon attempt after the layoff, I had hopes of something below 2:15. Instead, I stopped at thirteen miles, hands on my knees, stomach rebelling.

I was discouraged by the relapse, but by now I thought I had narrowed the problem down to two main things. First, stomach acid seemed to be present as an irritant. Second, an accumulation of phlegm at the back of the throat seemed to act as a trigger. For my next marathon attempt, at the Twin Cities, I took medication to inhibit the production of stomach acid.

But by ten miles I was thinking about my Buick.

By the time I abandoned that old car in California after repeated attempts at repair, I had learned an awful lot about how a car works. I had eliminated a few suspected causes in its flawed cooling system. (The thermostat, for example, was fine.) And after having learned so much about the problem, I was more determined than ever to find a solution. A new water pump didn't do the job. A new head gasket proved useless. Even a new engine didn't seem to help the car stay cool.

And similarly, after ten minutes of vomiting in Minneapolis, I was more angry than frustrated. I had thought the problem was solved. My stomach disagreed. But I knew I had to be closing in on the culprit. Stomach acid didn't seem to be the real problem. Diet and liquid aid were important, but not central. Heat and humidity were important issues, but was my thermostat really defective?

If you've ever agonized like this, searching for the key to an injury, a quirk, or some other flaw that upsets your running plans, you know how obsessive the quest becomes. After years of struggling with unsuccessful remedies, though, you begin to think that maybe there is no solution, only an inability of the body to perform the task at hand.

My newborn daughter, for example, has been unable to keep food down much of the time. Where most parents would say, "She has your eyes," or "She's got your nose," my wife says, "She's got your digestive system." After trying several things to help her keep the food down, we've finally discovered why she throws up so much. She has "gastroesophageal reflux." This means, of course, that she throws up a lot.

Is the solution, then, as easy as finding the right name? Do I have gastroesophageal reflux? Hearing a name for my daughter's malady put my mind at ease. Perhaps the solution for running problems could be as easy. Let's call those otherwise unnamed flaws in our human anatomy "zekes," "geeks," "weasels," or whatever. That way, instead of telling someone, "I feel sick to my stomach after running halfway through a marathon, and the feeling often leads to vomiting," I can just say, "I have a stomach zeke," or "I suffered from an intestinal geek at twenty miles." A friend of mine who has had groin pain that's kept him from running for two years can finally stop consulting doctors and offering multiple possibilities for what's wrong. From now on, he can just complain of having a severe groin weasel. Giving the problem a name may put him on the road to recovery.

Once again, though, I have my doubts. My daughter still throws up and, so far, so do I. Finding the name hasn't yet suggested a solution for either of us. Does the final episode of the Buick story offer guidance?

After virtually giving up on fixing the old car, I had resigned myself to driving only in cool weather for short periods of time. Within bounds, then, the car worked fine. Having accepted its fate as a short-distance vehicle, I stopped worrying about it.

As I got in the driver's seat one day, though, I felt a rush of inspiration. Had I ever really checked the radiator? I disconnected it and took it to a radiator specialist.

The most obvious solution of all turned out to be the right one. The lousy thing was so rusted inside that water could hardly circulate. That had been the root of the problem all along. But why hadn't I thought of it earlier?

I'm not sure I appreciated the full extent of the Buick's lesson as I stood on the side of the road in Minneapolis. I only remember the frustration of having another supposed solution prove ineffective. Back to the drawing board.

Now, though, I think the old car's message is clearer. It may be true that some problems, no matter who you consult or how hard you try, keep surfacing like whales, gigantic and immovable. And it may be that our flaws are irreparable. But sometimes, just when we've accepted them, a solution appears, simple and obvious. I hope so.

After the radiator was fixed, the car ran beautifully for years. May we all be so fortunate.

Collision Course

MOST of Stanford University's campus sits comfortably, sedately, on flatland. Classrooms, libraries, dormitories, and athletic facilities are almost all built on a small segment of Leland Stanford's old 8000-acre farm, a parcel that belies the true geography of the area. One does not need to venture far to notice a change.

To the west, a five-minute run brings the beginning of foothills that separate the San Francisco Bay Area from the Pacific Ocean and from the atrocious fog-banks characteristic of the coast.

Like the first tiny scratchings of an EKG recording of an awakening heartbeat, the hills behind the university signal the beginning of larger foothills, the pulse of different landforms and an active geological region. The San Andreas Fault is nearby.

We spent little time, as Stanford distance runners, in the flatlands. Typically, we headed for the hills.

In the late sixties, the running boom was unborn. We ran, solitary figures, through the Stanford outback, enjoying our loneliness, our camaraderie, our competitive urgings, and our association with the hills. The schizophrenic hills, with their combination of cows and radiotelescopes, horses and antennas, angry farmers and engineers, had not made up their minds what, exactly, they were. Neither had we.

And who were "we"? We were members of the Stanford cross-country team. Members today of a common collegiate mythology only "we," I suppose, can enjoy.

We were Arvid Kretz, a delicately constructed music major who was stopped by police while running late at night dressed in white shirt, black slacks, black shoes, and white socks, carrying his alto sax. In the middle of a run home from music practice, Arvid had trouble convincing the police of his membership on the Stanford track team. For a week, he was the prime suspect in the robbery of a nearby health spa.

We were "Large" Al Sanford, who joined and quit the team at least four times, usually in futile attempts to improve his social life. A horribly embarrassing episode, in which a fragrant love letter, composed, perfumed, and delivered to his mailbox by "friends" on the team, led him to open his heart to the girl who supposedly wrote the note, ranks at the top of a long list of Large Al stories. Nowadays, "Large" usually tells the stories himself.

We were Dan Cautley, a middle-distance runner and *Dragnet* devotee who once, on the way home from a movie, walked up to the first-floor window of a late-night student, showed him his ID, and said, "Hello, I'm Officer Friday. I'd like to ask you a few questions." The student was unamused and Dan left, but the next morning he got a call from a real police detective. The officer had found the ID, which Dan had inadvertently dropped, outside the window. A stereo system had been stolen from one of the dorm rooms, and Dan's ID on the ground suggested his involvement. Dan explained about *Dragnet*, Officer Joe Friday, and his routine the night before at the student's window. The real officer listened intently during the intricate explanation.

"That's the best story I've ever heard," he finally said. "And I don't believe a word of it."

Dan, like Arvid, became a prime robbery suspect.

We were Tom Teitge, who ran workouts with his dachshund, Wolfgang. Tom received his diploma from Stanford dressed as Captain America, proudly flashing his garbage-can lid to an appreciative commencement gathering.

We were Brook Thomas, articulate, cynical, and cheap. A student of literature and mooching, Brook once spent a summer camped in the bushes behind one of Stanford's dorms, his clothes hung neatly on hangers in the branches.

And we were Brook's older brother Ramsay, a fugitive from medical school, history grad school, and the Peace Corps, who had competed well in middle-distance events at the University of Mary-

land. Ramsay, in the throes of indecision as to his future, came west
to spend time at Stanford, and ended up sleeping in late most mornings and napping most afternoons in Brook's dorm room. When it
finally came time to have letters of recommendation written for a
new career possibility, Ramsay asked Brook to fill one out. In answer
to the question, "In what position did you know the applicant?"
Brook dutifully wrote, "Horizontal."

All in all, we were an extended family with a common interest
in competitive distance running. We spent a good portion of our
college years honing our racing skills, searching for the right combination of speed and endurance, ingredients that could produce
personal records and team victories. We enjoyed ourselves immensely.

Training in the hills behind the university, we often traveled
Sand Hill Road, running parallel to the Stanford Linear Accelerator
Center, or "SLAC." SLAC looked like a two-mile-long garage with
a cluster of large buildings on one end. It seemed perfectly level and
perfectly bizarre in a flat section of the field next to Sand Hill Road.
Occasionally we saw white-tailed deer nearby. When we ran next
to SLAC, it seemed to take a long, long time.

In the collegiate climate of the late sixties, we were distrustful
of the damned thing, which seemed to be an offspring of the unhealthy relationship between government and academia. Since no
one, or at least no one I knew, seemed to be able to explain what
went on at SLAC, speculation about its purpose ran wild. It was
an atom smasher. It used as much electricity as the whole Bay Area.
It had something to do with radioactivity or weapons or something.
It was certainly dangerous. None of the myths in particular, though,
seemed to stand the test of time. After the student unrest of the
sixties began to ease, while I spent my last year in the area before
moving back to Seattle, suspicion of SLAC was replaced by a different response.

There should be a race around the thing.

Whenever I found myself running near the facility, I enjoyed
the notion of what a SLAC road race would be like. A two-mile
straightaway, one turn, a two-mile backstretch. No hills, no scenery.

Racing the electrons. Accelerating, using energy, hitting the wall.

It never happened. With the facility off-limits to the public, with the kind of secretive and dangerous (or so we thought) work scientists did there, there seemed little chance of something as frivolous as a road race being allowed nearby.

I left the Stanford hills, most of my college friends, and SLAC behind in 1972 to return to Seattle.

"What is this race?" Brook asked me. "Nobody I've asked seems to know anything about it."

"It's not a race," I corrected him. "It's a fun-run. Around SLAC."

Brook scowled and said something I can't seem to remember.

It was August 15, 1980, two days before Ramsay's wedding, when "Large" would stand watching and comment, "Ramsay getting married. . . . This is quite an event."

To which one of the guys, one of the old friends, would add, "It's the end of an era. The sixties are finally over."

We would all laugh.

Brook and I were running, chasing trails in the Stanford hills that he had shown me for the first time more than ten years earlier. Now, though, we weren't solitary figures. A steady line of joggers, like a path of ants, wound up into the hills from the campus, past the cows, past the radiotelescope, over the sacred paths of our collegiate days.

To Brook, the hordes of other runners in the world are distressing. I sense that he tries to erase them from his perception, to focus on his own form, his own breathing, his own thoughts, and his own attempts at maintaining quickness during a run.

The trendiness of running, the media hype, the self-indulgence and narrow-mindedness of many new runners appall him.

"If I were in high school now," he once said, "I know I wouldn't turn out for cross-country. I'd do something else."

To Brook, I think, running is a skill to be sharpened, an engrossing but not overwhelming part of life, and an activity that should have been kept a secret among friends, not shouted from the tops of the Stanford hills to people who might not understand.

I was intentionally irking him when I called the run around SLAC, the run that I had once thought improbable but which was now scheduled for the same weekend as his brother Ramsay's wedding, a fun-run. Because Brook the racer feels the same way about fun-runs as Brook the English professor would feel about a Comics as Literature class. A waste of time.

We continued to run quickly up and down the hills, passing joggers and discussing our current lives, loves, and hopes, until I thought I could ask the question.

"Are you going to run at SLAC Sunday?"

Brook hesitated. I'm not sure what he was thinking, but I imagined he was trying to decide whether the SLAC run would be an event worthy of the sport or just a gathering of people uninterested in the upper realms of foot-speed.

"Maybe," he said at last. "I'll see."

"When I was in high school, I was intimidated by athletes."

The speaker was Carter B. Smith, an afternoon "jock" at KNBR radio in San Francisco. I was talking with him near the administrative offices at SLAC on the morning of the run, while a handful of people from KNBR and SLAC were getting things organized for the carloads of fun-runners who would soon arrive.

"I think a person can lead a complete, normal, happy life," he said, "without ever running."

Carter was baiting me, I realized. He knew my background, my interest in racing, my position with *Running* magazine. I found nothing wrong with his statement, though. I've said almost the same thing myself.

He looked at me with intense blue-gray eyes that could either smile or challenge. Now they challenged.

"I don't give a _____ if anyone runs or not."

I found myself liking this man a lot.

We were discussing KNBR's interest in running, their promotion of events like the SLAC run, and Carter B. Smith's own history as a runner.

"I've given up almost every vice a person can have," he told me.

"A few years ago I weighed two hundred and thirty pounds." I looked at him and, for the life of me, I could not imagine where he would hang all those pounds. "Now," he added, "I'm at a hundred and sixty." Thus spoke a man who cared not for running.

A few years ago one of the KNBR disc jockeys offhandedly invited listeners to join him for a run at a specified location on the weekend. The event was a success, the idea caught on, and soon the jocks had formed "The Amalgamated Joggers," a loose-knit collection of people interested in getting together for fun-runs at sites around the Bay Area. The station now helps sponsor one run a month.

"We've run at Angel Island," read the letter I received from Isabelle Lemon, KNBR and Amalgamated Joggers spokesperson, "a winery (we got chilled chenin blanc at the end of the run—now that's real class), a cheese factory, et cetera.

"But the general theme is fun. And the people who join us are super people. And we even had two Amalgamated Joggers who met at a run, subsequently got married, and we've never seen nor heard from them again."

Carter B. Smith and I were discussing his T-shirt collection, which is 1800 in number and growing daily, when his wife walked up. She was the only one of the organizers I had noticed who looked very worried about getting things organized.

"Where are the release forms?" she asked Carter. "And where are people supposed to sign them and who do I put in charge of that?"

"Those are all good questions," he replied, "none of which I know the answer to."

She was displeased with the response. Carter began helping her search for the release forms among the assorted containers of picnic foodstuffs. I switched my interviewing to Bob Adamson, a senior designer at SLAC and the man who helped put the event together.

Bob is a pleasant man who looks like *Bonanza*'s Ben Cartwright, even when he isn't wearing his cowboy hat. With the hat on, the similarity was distracting, and I had to keep reminding myself not to ask about Hoss and Little Joe. "God doesn't really like people," he told me. "You train like hell for a year, take three weeks off, and you're out of shape again."

He proceeded to tell me, in a patient, mellow voice, about his own association with running, his fortuitous association with a Stanford research team that was studying cardiovascular fitness, and his "membership" in The Amalgamated Joggers.

"They're a fun group," he told me. "That's the whole point. Fun."

"Did you have any trouble convincing the SLAC administrators to allow you to hold a fun-run here?" I asked, fishing for something.

"No. We don't do any classified work here," he responded. "There's no reason for them to object."

Reluctantly, I felt some of SLAC's mystique begin to fade. Nothing classified?

I turned suddenly, noticing a familiar face on the scene. Brook had arrived.

"You decided to run," I said, honestly surprised.

"I will if I wake up in time," he replied. He did a few half-hearted stretches and went to warm up.

I didn't tell Brook about my discussions with Carter, about Carter's contention that racing was counterproductive to what this event was all about. Nor did I tell Carter about Brook's feelings about fun-running. I just watched the two of them jogging and walking around, warming up. Opposite ends of the spectrum.

In a few minutes Brook and I were racing side by side down the longest straightaway I had ever seen, matching strides, leaving a mass of fun-runners behind.

The Stanford Linear Accelerator Center, as I discovered during a lecture after the run, was completed in 1966 at a cost of $114 million. It is a facility used by nuclear physicists to study the smallest particles of matter known to man, particles that are called "quarks" after an elusive fictional character in James Joyce's novel *Finnegans Wake*.

Quarks are smaller than molecules, smaller than atoms, smaller than neutrons or protons or electrons. Smaller, even, than Volkswagens or Datsuns.

"In high-energy physics you have to have bigger and bigger machines to see smaller and smaller things," SLAC's director, W. K. H. Panofsky, once remarked. The statement suggests a distortion of logic with which physicists seem to be at home in making sense out of elementary particle research.

Scientists use SLAC today to study particles that were totally unknown to man ten years ago when I first began running the Stanford hills.

"Actually," said our tour guide, a theoretical physicist named Bruce Sawhill, "what you ran around today was a government hiding of a two-mile-long KNBR antenna." We laughed, and Bruce went on to explain what he and his cohorts were trying to do at SLAC.

It went something like this: Physicists use different kinds of accelerators for different kinds of research. For a while, they bombarded known elements with accelerated electrons to produce new elements. Unfortunately, though, most of the new elements were around for less time than William Henry Harrison. The physicists lost interest in atom smashing after a few good collisions.

Later, facilities like SLAC were conceived and constructed because, unlike circular accelerators, in which electrons lose energy going around turns (like runners on an indoor track), the linear path allows electrons to be accelerated at speeds more closely approaching (to within .00000001 percent) the speed of light.

Einstein taught us that anything going that fast increases in mass. The accelerated electrons at SLAC are 40,000 times more massive than the ones that make your socks stick together in the dryer. When they collide with something, they hit hard.

For a while, scientists used SLAC electrons to bombard protons, trying to bust the little buggers apart. They were unsuccessful, but in the process they determined the existence of the first three quarks, which they called "up," "down," and "strange." Later, "charm" was identified.

A major adjustment occurred at SLAC in 1972, when the accelerated electrons and their antimatter buddies, the positrons, were separated at the end of the two-mile tunnel and sent in opposite directions around a circular vacuum tube and finally made to collide. In the resulting pure explosion of matter and antimatter, electron and positron, a fifth and sixth quark were identified.

"They were originally named 'truth' and 'beauty,' " Bruce told us, "from a poem that says that truth and beauty cannot be found in this world. Later, it was decided that that was a little obnoxious, and they were renamed 'top' and 'bottom.' "

The final change in the SLAC design was the addition, in 1978, of an enormous circular ring many times larger than the one installed in 1972. Now, electrons and positrons are accelerated near the speed of light down the linear accelerator, sent in opposite directions around the larger, more efficient storage ring, and made to collide with even greater explosive energy. Truth and beauty sometimes result.

We left the lecture room and boarded buses for a tour of the facility. As we headed along the path of that morning's run, Bruce explained that the actual accelerator tunnel was well underground. The part we ran next to, the two-mile-long "garage," is actually housing for the klystron gallery. Klystrons are machines that emit huge bursts of microwave energy, accelerating the electrons, as Bruce told us, "like waves accelerating surfers."

We ended our tour by viewing the collision end of the facilities, where one of the runners asked, "Is there a military use for any of this?"

We were assured that there was not, that SLAC was engaged in pure research, in spite of the fact that accelerators were being studied elsewhere for possible military application.

I refrained from saying so, but in my heart I was glad to know that if accelerators were ever aimed at the sky, at least I was privileged to have the klystrons on my side.

The tour ended, the crowd dispersed, the KNBR picnic was winding down. Brook had left a long time ago.

How was I to make sense of all this?

I had had a weekend of nostalgia and high-energy physics. Racing and fun-running. Was there, somewhere, as in scientists' attempts to find a common ground among the diverse forces known to physics, a synthesis of it all?

There had been no terrible collision between the opposite philosophies of fun-running and racing that day. Was it too obnoxious to think that if there had been, truth and beauty would have resulted? Or would we even have known up from down?

I thought back to the race. Brook and I were charging down the accelerator homestretch, following the path of the electron beam, clipping along at five minutes a mile. The straightaway seemed endless, and suddenly we seemed to be running in a moment of suspended time.

Brook and I, friends for years, who had raced each other countless times, were racing again. In that moment, while we struggled to achieve the top speeds our bodies would allow, we also ran for Stanford teammates who weren't there with us. We ran together, straining against limitations, trying to discover something elemental about life.

I glanced over at Brook, and I thought of something that had once happened to me at a Sunday fun-run back in Spokane. The organizer had always stressed health, cardiovascular fitness, and easy running, and was dismayed at those of us who ran fast.

On that morning he cornered me after the run, striving to be good-natured, and said, "What are you doing, running like that? This is a fun-run, you know."

I looked at him, and said words that came back to me as Brook and I sprinted along the electron path at SLAC.

"It's fun to run fast," I told him.

Brook and I, fast fun-runners or fun fast-runners, ex-members of the Stanford cross-country team, went on to finish the SLAC run together, sprinting at a speed considerably slower than accelerated electrons.

He left almost immediately to take a nap.

I stayed to take in a tour of the SLAC facilities and enjoy a picnic lunch, graciously supplied by The Amalgamated Joggers.

Confessions of a Nutritional Agnostic

"I'M AN ATHEIST with one foot in the door of agnosticism," said Woody Allen. "I don't believe in an afterlife, but I do plan to take along a change of shorts."

Most of the top runners I know feel the same way about diet. They're skeptical of nutrition being the prime element in racing success, but they like to check each other's grocery lists. Just in case.

When I was a freshman in college, I read an article on one of the quarter-milers on our team, who was known for racing well on limited training. When asked what his secret was, he said, "I owe it all to my diet."

This, the notion that you could eat your way to success or failure, became a team joke. "I lost it at the dinner table," and "I was carrying too much excess baggage, so to speak," became excuses for poor performances. After college, when I suddenly lopped twenty seconds off my three-mile best, a reporter asked me how I explained the sudden improvement. The old joke came to mind.

"I owe it all to my diet," I told him. And I went on to describe a typical day's food intake: Froot Loops and orange juice for breakfast, peanut butter and jelly sandwiches and cookies for lunch, pizza and beer for dinner. I wasn't making this up, by the way.

My diet made the pages of a national magazine, not once but several times afterward, and my reputation as a nutritional junkie has followed me around like a jackal ever since. I've been both a dietary pariah among runners with nutritional sensibilities and something of a hero to the dietary unconscious. I've been justly scorned by true nutritional believers, awarded boxes of Froot Loops by race organizers, and made privy to the worst nutritional confessions imaginable.

While attending a running camp where only nutritionally sound food was served, I was hustled aside one morning by a man who told me, while his gaze darted nervously back and forth across the landscape for the approach of the camp director, of having driven to town the evening before for a hot fudge sundae.

"I thought you'd appreciate hearing about it," he said, after describing his transgression in great dripping detail. I was, so it seemed, his sucrose soul-mate.

I'm not sure I deserve the reputation. My diet has always been eclectic and ethnically balanced. As a fast-food dilettante, I have dabbled in burgers, fried chicken, burritos, pizza, and barbecued rice. I graze in my backyard amid strawberries, tomatoes, carrots, potatoes, and pea pods. At meals, I eat everything in sight, and there is generally someone with better nutritional insight than mine supplying the options.

But it is between meals, I suppose, that I lose control and earn my reputation. Cookies, crackers, cakes, pies, pastries, pop, and beer are all devoured and guzzled, but chief among my weaknesses is ice cream.

As a child, I would sit in front of the television after dinner with an enormous bowl of chocolate mint chip or fudge swirl, joyously playing with my dessert, whipping the chocolate in with the vanilla, digging caverns into the side of the frozen mountain, and consuming mouthful after mouthful until, inevitably, I had to leave the room to put on a wool sweater. Then it was time for a second helping.

In college, I did not outgrow this habit. Many times my teammates tried to rescue me from supposedly lethal helpings of ice cream and hot fudge on evenings before important races. Or so they said, though the indulgence never seemed to bother my performance. And even now, well into my adult life, I am impressive in wrestling with a Mount Everest, Pig Trough, or whatever specialty concoction an ice cream establishment may set in front of me. I just have to remember to dress warmly.

I know I'm not alone among runners in harboring this sort of passion for caloric excess, nor in generally adhering to a less than model diet. It's not unusual to hear runners justify the time they spend exercising as a balance to the time they spend eating, especially eating unwisely. More than one running club I know of would be more appropriately termed an eating club. But whatever their dietary sins, most runners, even the top competitors, don't seem to believe they're doing themselves much harm.

It's not unusual to see runners before a marathon loading with all manner of "good" and "bad" carbohydrates, but this kind of loading is almost as common at other times as well. After the 1980 Honolulu Marathon, I went with a group of Nike runners that included Patti Catalano to a restaurant we had enjoyed the previous year. The headwaiter immediately recognized our group.

"Is that girl who had three desserts last year back?" he asked. Patti blushed.

At a study of competitive distance runners conducted at the Aerobics Clinic in Dallas in 1975, Frank Shorter was taken aside by Kenneth Cooper and urged to improve his diet. The body, Frank was told, is like a race car that needs high-grade fuel to perform at its peak. Frank had been filling his high-performance body with low-octane fuel. Junk food.

"I know your times would improve if you would improve your diet," said Dr. Cooper. "Someday I'll prove it to you. Someday," he concluded with a smile, "they'll award me the Nobel Prize for proving it."

"The Pulitzer Prize, maybe," responded Frank, "for fiction."

Top runners, of course, are not always immune to the attractions of diet in the quest for excellence. If dietary intake can improve performance by even a small percentage, so the theory goes, then it's worth serious consideration. If nutrition is responsible for even the minutest of advantages in otherwise equally endowed, equally trained, equally motivated athletes, then it will spell the difference between victory and defeat. Or, as Masters runner Alex Ratelle has said, "What do I eat before a race? I'll tell you what I eat. I eat whatever the guy who finished ahead of me in the last race ate."

Ratelle's quip has an unmistakable ring of truth about it, suggesting the quest for The Secret, a magical formula for athletic success, the fountain of fastness. "Eat what the winner eats" is a motto that has set more athletic eating trends than science will ever encourage. This is not necessarily good news.

As competitors, we seem able, on the one hand, to believe that training is the deciding element of success while on the other hand suspecting that the other guy might be hiding something from us. A particular foodstuff in the closet, perhaps, or a vitamin supplement under the napkin? What is that powder he's dumping in the blender? We are both amused and fascinated by our suspicions.

At last count, Lasse Viren had revealed four key Nordic secrets on various occasions in response to media questions about how he had won all those gold medals. Lasse's secrets? Reindeer milk, reindeer meat, reindeer blood, and reindeer excrement—the first three being key elements of his diet, the last rubbed judiciously on his legs right before the race. He was kidding, of course—wasn't he?

There is a natural tendency, in fact, for people to assume that an athlete of Lasse's talents must have something going for him other than superb conditioning, tactics, and motivation. Blood-doping or reindeer blood, perhaps, but something must be giving him the edge, right?

Most dieticians are dubious of there being any sort of miracle food to improve athletic performance, although this hasn't stopped athletes from trying a whole host of dietary tricks. Whether it's wheat germ, spirulina algae, bee pollen, or vitamin supplements, there are always plenty of athletic advocates around to sing the praises.

Among dietary tricks for runners, though, the undisputed heavyweight champion of the world would have to be carbohydrate loading. Discovered by cross-country skiers as a way of increasing glycogen storage in the muscles, the technique of depletion and loading has been widely used among marathon runners to improve endurance. Though there are many, myself included, who continue to use the system, there are also plenty of detractors around to point out the risks and complications of drastically altering the diet.

"I tried depleting once," Frank Shorter said at a clinic I attended a few years ago. "But after one day I started seeing double, so I went and had a handful of M&Ms and a couple of beers and felt fine. I've never depleted since."

Frank is not the only runner to have given up the severe depletion phase of carbo loading. Whether to avoid shock to the system or problems around home and work, many runners have modified the scheme, depleting in moderation or not at all, but still loading with reckless abandon. Personally, I feel that if you haven't suffered through the three days of weakness, ill manners, and suicidal depression that characterize depletion, you don't deserve to go into a marathon with extra glycogen.

Aside from the notion of a secret food or dietary trick, most people believe that athletes must generally eat differently than the rest of society. In spite of evidence to the contrary, athletes are believed to shun most of the foods that other people enjoy. A few years ago, the most common line runners heard was probably, "Ten miles a day? I don't even drive ten miles a day." Now, the thing I keep hearing is, "What's a runner doing eating that?"

And what is "that"? Beer, soft drinks, tacos, pizza, ice cream, cookies, et cetera. In short, all the good stuff. And not all of it, by the way, deserves to be titled "junk food." Pizza and tacos, for example, aren't badly balanced according to most dieticians, and even my beloved ice cream has its share of nutritional advocates. But the general public continues to believe that athletes avoid these kinds of foods. Perhaps some do. But not many.

It may be true that athletes eat differently than the rest of society, though not in the way most people assume. High-mileage runners seem to be able to satisfy basic nutritional requirements because they eat a lot. As Dr. William Bennett says in *The Dieter's Dilemma*, "One of the wonderful things about exercise is that it allows the body to take over the job of weight control, so that you can eat more and automatically expose yourself to more nutrients, such as vitamins and minerals." Or, twisting Bennett's words to fit my own beliefs, one might say that even the runner who lives on Ding-Dongs and beer must occasionally consume apples and oranges. Voracious caloric intake demands it.

In fact, exercise seems to have several advantages for those who want to avoid restricting their diet. It burns calories, may suppress appetite, and, it is now believed, acts through the brain to modify the body's metabolic rate. Peter Wood and other researchers at Stanford University have shown that runners typically consume more calories than their sedentary counterparts and yet weigh significantly less. Fat people aren't gluttons, runners are. This is not news, of course, to our nonrunning friends and relatives who have seen us in action.

Still, the general public have seen so many commercials with trim athletes eating low-calorie foods that they've actually begun to believe that that's what they eat. The simple fact that carbohydrates are the main nutritional accomplice of exercising athletes has had trouble finding acceptance in many quarters, mainly because of the emphasis on protein in dietary advertising.

When sugar-free sodas and light beers first began to show up sponsoring road races in the mid-seventies, many runners were incredulous. "Can anyone tell me," asked one runner at a prerace clinic sponsored by a light beer company at about that time, "what a bunch of ectomorphs like ourselves are doing sitting around drinking diet beer and low-cal pop?"

The beauties of carbohydrates, though, are finally being given their due, and the legion of carbo supporters is continuing to grow. Researchers at MIT have recently shown that eating carbohydrates may raise the level of a particular chemical in the brain, thereby lessening depression and sensitivity to pain, as well as inducing calmness, relaxation, and sleepiness. I've known this, more or less, all my life.

Moreover, the whole insistence on avoiding sugar has come under fire in recent years, especially when the alternatives may be more harmful than the sweet stuff itself. William Bennett (a man who is rapidly heading to the top of my "Top Ten Nutritional Counselors" list) has more to say on the subject in an article in *American Health*, where he contends that fat and sedentary lifestyles, and not sugar, are the main culprits of obese America.

"Choosing to drink a diet cola instead of a sugar-sweetened one is a strategy designed to avoid walking about a mile and a half," he says. "But the tactic would only work if artificial sweeteners actually *replaced* sugar in the diet. Instead, artificial sweeteners seem merely to provide an additional source of sweet taste that appeals to an inborn appetite but does not truly satisfy it." And so on.

I may be accused at this point of being capricious in quoting nutritional research and information, of having chosen what supports my eating habits while ignoring the rest. In doing so I'm in good company.

A whopping big serving of nutritional information seems to be based more on wishful thinking than on science. Nutritional information and advice seem to change more often than the weather, and when they do, science is usually to blame. Someone finally decides to do some testing.

The best recent example of that is the "complex" carbohydrate escapade. After years of hearing that "simple" carbohydrates like glucose, sucrose, and fructose enter the bloodstream too quickly, thereby causing a rapid rise in blood sugar and blood insulin, while "complex" carbos like the starches found in rice and potatoes do not, Phyllis Crapo of the University of Denver Health Sciences Center decided to test the theory. The result has been a dramatic reversal of nutritional dogma. Some "complex" carbohydrates, she found, like those in white potatoes, whole-wheat or white bread, and cooked carrots, are worse than sucrose in raising blood sugar levels.

"Potatoes are like candy as far as a diabetic is concerned," concludes coresearcher Jerrold Olefsky. And since every "complex" carbohydrate gives a different glucose response, we'll have to stay tuned to find out who the good guys and bad guys are in this episode.

This sort of nutritional revisionism, I suppose, should not be cause for despair. It is, thankfully, the melody of science, which seems to be a relative Johnny-come-lately in nutritional discussions. And while science spends its days carefully testing hypotheses, I plan to spend mine eating, drinking, and running merrily, knowing that nutritional information is progressing by leaps and bounds, although probably not fast enough to save me.

And in the meantime, for those of you who seem to want rules of diet to live by, I offer you ten of my own, developed during a third of a century of conscientious consumption. Not science, of course, just the deranged preachings of a nutritional agnostic.

I urge you to consider them, though, in spite of warnings from the American Dietetic Association about excess sodium in the diet, with a grain of salt:

1. If it's labeled "healthy" or "natural," or any derivative thereof, hold onto your wallet and run for cover—Real natural food grows in your garden and has bugs and worms all over it. "Natural" shouldn't necessarily be considered a compliment. Think of natural disaster, natural childbirth, et cetera, before you buy anything "natural."

2. If you run one hundred miles a week, you can eat anything you want—Why? Because (a) you'll burn all the calories you consume, (b) you deserve it, and (c) you'll be injured soon and back on a restricted diet anyway.

3. There is no such thing as a bad carbohydrate, with the possible exception of squash. Carbohydrates are all good, though some of them, of course, are guilty of causing roller-coaster swings in blood sugar levels and rotting your teeth.

4. There is no such thing as a complex carbohydrate. If carbohydrates were complex, they wouldn't answer to such a pretentious name. They would have been satisfied with a name like "protein" or a supremely overconfident moniker like "fat," which is a substance complex enough not to have to prove it with a four-syllable title.

5. Avoid carbohydrate loading when friends or relatives are in town. During depletion you'll insult them, during loading you'll disgust them.

6. Drinking two cups of coffee shortly before starting a marathon will help release free fatty acids into the bloodstream. I don't know exactly what they are or what they do, but at least they're free.

7. Avoid any diet that discourages the use of hot fudge.

8. If you eat foods that are half as nutritious as they should be, eat twice as much.

9. Whatever substance you're being encouraged to take in large doses today will be found to be carcinogenic within six months.

10. Without ice cream there would be chaos and darkness.

Dropping Out

THE FLIGHT to Europe had begun with a teddy bear, but was rapidly degenerating into Texans.

We had left Spokane, Dan and I, sitting across from a teenage girl cuddling her teddy, some vague recollection of familiarity and security connecting her to the ground, its tattered and weary face no longer beaming joy to the little girl who had first welcomed it to her bed. Now ole teddy had been dragged along against his will onto an airplane, and he obviously wasn't enjoying himself. He had performed noble service in bringing his mistress to the edge of adulthood, but now, by God, he deserved a rest! Not some fool trip on an airplane with a girl old enough to be someone's mother.

Some people, I thought, looking at the poor captive, just don't know when it's time to move on.

And then we picked up a load of Texans, who could not possibly have been as stupid as they acted. Seemingly within minutes of taking off from Kennedy Airport, the whole lot of them were drunk. They became creatures with the bodies of manatees and the personalities of jackals.

"Bob's bar is open for business!" one bellowed, staggering in the aisle.

"Hey, look at Animal!" another shouted, beaming at one of his friends in the back of the plane. "That boy's tryin' to sleep. Hey, Animal!"

Yuk, yuk.

It was, coincidentally, the middle of the night. Animal and the rest of us *were* trying to sleep. But like most slobbering-drunk, gorilla-brained packs of good old boys, this group thought they were entertaining everyone within eyesight and earshot. Most countries have enough sense to sequester their insipid inebriates in dark corners of the land where they can eventually eliminate each other fighting

48

over who can spit the farthest. The U.S.A. was apparently sending some of theirs abroad with pocketsful of oil money to act as good-will ambassadors.

I slunk down in my seat and tried to ignore them.

The question of what I was doing on this airborne oil rig was a good one, especially in view of the discomfort I was enduring. Months earlier I had been invited to run the Frankfurt Marathon, much to my excitement and dismay. Excitement, of course, because I would be able to take a road trip to Germany, with as many excursions to bordering countries as time, good sense, energy, and money would allow. Dismay, because I would have to run another marathon.

You see, I was rapidly becoming disenchanted with marathons.

While the Texans railed on about how much they could drink, I closed my eyes and reflected on my last two serious marathon efforts. Last November, Rio de Janeiro. I had enjoyed a week in one of the finest places on earth, a truly cosmopolitan city designed to be picturesque and playful. Rio is spread among the enormous rock-bunions, stone-blisters, and boulder-corns of some huge granite giant's foot, the big toe of Sugarloaf pointing at the sky. The scenery is unbeatable. The beaches are a tribute to hedonism. The women are alluring and intriguing. To marathon here does not make sense.

Nevertheless Jose Werneck, a local sportswriter and broadcaster, had caught marathon fever in the states and was determined to see it spread to his homeland. Tapping insistently on the shoulder of the *Jornal do Brasil*, his employer, he was finally able to convince his bosses to host a major marathon through the streets of Rio. Everyone, including Jose, was amazed when over a thousand runners showed up one warm evening to take a shot at forty-two kilometers.

The race time was planned to take advantage of the setting sun. We began in the late afternoon, as thousands of people were heading home from a hard day at the beach.

One must admire the courage of Jose and the other organizers in trying to direct hundreds of runners through city streets filled with Latin drivers. Rio is a city of tunnels, turns, and traffic, a nightmare for footracers. As we wove our way along the first few miles, we were asked to stay in the right lane for safety. Meanwhile,

cars honked, motorists yelled, engines revved, and motorcycles buzz-
sawed their way down the lanes next to us. Pedestrians stepped in
front of runners and bicycles swerved between them.

Greg Meyer, leading the way through this maelstrom, nearly
collided with several of the bicycles that surrounded him during the
race. Edson Bergara, a Brazilian runner, was running well in second
place when a motorcycle ran over his foot, and he had to stop for a
few minutes. All the runners had trouble breathing in the exhaust-
infused tunnels. The noise was overwhelming.

Except for missing out on water at the first station, I survived
the first twenty-five kilometers with minimal discomfort, considering
the obstacles. It was impossible to feel relaxed, but at least I was
progressing normally toward the finish, running a solid though lack-
luster race. One does not recognize the progressive effects of dehydration, though, until one is a veritable prune, a camel with shriveled
hump, a sun-bleached desert-mummy. Though it wasn't warm by
Brazilian standards, by thirty kilometers I was in heat trouble.

Or so I thought. Maybe it was glycogen depletion or lack of
training or jet lag or bad attitude. All I really know is that I was
dizzy, exhausted, sore, tight, and dry as I hobbled the last few
kilometers along Ipanema and Copacabana beaches, with two large
blood blisters on my feet and a dagger-stitch in my side, whimpering
and mumbling to myself. A guy rode up on his bike and assured
me that if I kept going I would get third. I got sixth.

My hosts were understanding. They were pleased with having
put on Brazil's largest marathon, determined to correct the mistakes
they had made, and seemingly unconcerned with my having performed poorly. I, on the other hand, was embarassed to have flown
so far to have run so shoddily. The warmth of the Brazilian people
and the Brazilian weather had made for a great trip, but what was
the point of the marathon?

"I'm gonna give that girl a kiss!" one of the Texans was telling
his friend, loudly, as the stewardess walked by.

"She's a cold one, she is," the other replied. "I wouldn't bother,
if I was you."

Thankfully, neither did, and I returned to my personal reverie.

Last March, Tokyo. All my life, or at least since I've been marathoning, I've wanted to run in Japan. After the Montreal Olympics, I thought I'd have a chance at an invitation to run Fukuoka. None came. Years passed.

Then, out of nowhere in particular, I received an invitation to run the Tokyo/New York Friendship Marathon, sponsored by the Fuji-Sankei broadcasting conglomerate. I was soon whisked, slippered, through the accommodating skies of Japan Airlines to Tokyo, where I was interviewed and photographed at Narita Airport. The other passengers stared in puzzlement.

"What was that all about?" one of the Americans from the flight asked me as we waited to go through customs. "Are you someone famous?"

"I run marathons. The Japanese love marathons."

Indeed they do. And they treat their guests, marathon or otherwise, uncommonly well. Whether they're offering food, drink, gifts, or assistance through the maze of incomprehensible Japanese signs and symbols in Tokyo subway stations, they treat outsiders well. As a result, I enjoyed my visit there.

I enjoyed the Japanese love of gadgetry, whereby every room becomes an empty space to be lit, wired, and secured with every conceivable kind of device. My modest hotel room contained smoke alarms, three sprinklers, a thermometer, doorbell, TV, refrigerator, radio, alarm clock, heater, air conditioner, and a telephone with an extension in the bathroom. And lamps: ceiling lamps, foot lamps, telephone lamps, a reading lamp with a smaller dim lamp with fluorescent knobs, lamps in the bathroom and the closet, and a flashlight in case all the other lamps went off. The light in the closet lit up automatically when the door was opened, and the light switches were illuminated when all the other lights were out. The radio played the sound of birds chirping for an hour each morning, and more than once I was awakened by a telephone call replete with those bird sounds, played for my benefit by Herm Atkins, Benji Durden, or one of the other runners on hand for the marathon.

And of course I enjoyed spending time with those other runners. Like Herm, who heard me tell Durden, as Benji was lining up french fries on a hamburger bun for a carbohydrate sandwich, that that was the kind of bizarre activity that might end up in a magazine article, and who proceeded to line up french fries on his own hamburger bun. Okay, Herm, you made it into the magazine, just like I told you.

Like Chris Stewart, the irrepressible British runner, whose lines like "My, but aren't you a squishy ball of delight" are so outlandish as to prove effective on ladies of various persuasions. "How can I kiss you if you're so tall?" Chris told us he had asked an American girl down South a few months earlier. "She just smiled, patted me on the head, and gave me a bagel."

Like Gary Fanelli, whose subtle wit was generally lost in translation. "Mexicans have a good altitude on running, at least in Mexico City" and "Finland really made the greatest contribution to distance running—the Finnish line" and "Seiko's the man to watch" were all about as funny as puns ever are, but his cry of "Hey, Elwood!" upon seeing IAAF magnate Adrian Paulen walk by, an obscure reference to the Blues Brothers, was largely lost on the old boy, although it did cause him to stop and shake Fanelli's hand.

And I enjoyed the fervor with which the Japanese embark on a marathon venture, whether it's the constant media attention or the joyous celebration. They handle every detail with a care and precision that suggests their high regard for the sport. In Japan, marathoning is a major event, not something that sprouted in the dark when no one was looking.

So I enjoyed Japanese hospitality, Japanese culture, spending time with other runners, and the whole atmosphere of the event. And then came the race.

I was not without my excuses. I had come to Japan with a weak arch in my right foot, and it had bothered me on every training run. Beyond that, I had strained a neck muscle a few days earlier, and it was still difficult to move my head. For good measure, I had bitten my tongue.

In spite of these precautions, I felt I might be obliged to turn in a good performance if I ran conservatively in the cool weather. At least I wouldn't be wrestling with the heat as I had in Rio. We began the race in Tokyo's Olympic stadium and were soon traveling the city streets, where thousands of fans waved flags and shouted encouragement.

While Benji, Herm, Randy Thomas, Rodolfo Gomez, Tommy Persson, and a few others were battling for the lead during the first half of the race, I moved steadily through the field farther back, hoping to finish well. Until thirty kilometers I felt fine. From thirty to thirty-two, my body began breaking out in question marks. At thirty-two kilometers, the bubble burst, the sack broke, and the bottom dropped out of my race. I made it to forty kilometers because I knew there would be syrupy orange juice there. I stopped and drank three glasses. I made it to the finish because I knew there was a box lunch waiting for me, and I imagined chocolate cake. There was none.

During my stop at forty kilometers, while I stood silently consuming one orange juice after another, I remembered watching a movie of the Tokyo Olympics, where a Japanese runner had done almost exactly the same thing. We in the theater audience had laughed in delight. Now I was in the movie, and the Japanese audience around me was beginning to chuckle as I began downing my third cup. Thus was irony having the last laugh, though I couldn't have cared less. My bloodstream needed sugar.

It was the clearest, most isolated case of glycogen depletion I have ever experienced, and it was horrible. Afterward, I sat eating a sandwich in a room below the stadium, wishing I had never heard of the marathon. Rodolfo Gomez had won, Tommy Persson had finished second, Randy Thomas third, Benji Durden fourth, and I had hit the Tokyo wall. All the sake and Kirin beer in Japan, most of which I tried to consume that evening, did not lift my spirits. Again I had flown a long way to run poorly.

As I flew home a couple of days later, I did some serious soul-searching. Did I train properly? Did I load correctly? Did I pace myself intelligently? Was I too old? Not interested enough? Should I quit marathons? Quit running altogether? Or what?

Before the marathon I had made the decision that, due to the cool weather, I would avoid taking fluids at the aid stations. My stomach is sensitive to having anything added during a race, and I avoid taking fluids if it seems feasible. Yet if I had taken juice early in the Tokyo race, perhaps I would have delayed hitting the wall or avoided it altogether. Too much fluid and I might throw up, as I had done in three previous marathons. Not enough and I might hit the wall. I asked myself: Is throwing up worse than hitting the wall?

After a while, several things became clear. One, the attraction of wanting to run with the best runners in the world was still strong in my psyche. There would be no resorting to the life of a fun-runner. Two, I would recommit myself to a serious training regimen, with intervals and long runs. Three, I would go through the entire carbohydrate loading diet, including depletion, prior to my next marathon in Frankfurt. In spite of the difficulty of finding enough pure protein while in another country, in spite of the absurdity of being in Europe and having to avoid the native cuisine, and in spite of the overall stress, ill humor, and bad manners associated with depleting, I would do it.

And now, confident that dedicated carbo loading would be the key to my race in Frankfurt, I rode the plane to Europe with my photographer friend Dan Leahy, a carry-on bag filled with beef jerky, and a load of drunk Texans, one of whom was trying to get to his seat behind me but was listing badly to starboard.

A moment later, the bastard spilled nearly his entire glass of rum and coke on my sleeve. A bad omen.

As usual, the prerace travel was going well. Dan and I spent several days in Amsterdam, interviewing some of the top Dutch runners, sightseeing, and dodging traffic. The weather was cooperative and the people we met were accommodating. It was as enjoyable as Rio and Tokyo had been before the gun fired.

On our second day in Amsterdam, I stopped eating carbohydrates. For the remainder of the depletion days, I ate nuts, cheese, and beef jerky and stared ruefully in the windows of bakeries and chocolate shops. Dan agreed not to make loud noises of appreciation while eating Dutch chocolates, or at least to be out of earshot when he did so.

On the final day of depletion, I went on a long, slow run through one of Amsterdam's parks, while my head buzzed in anticipation of my first good carbo load the next morning. Down deep, I was pleased at having avoided temptation and sure it would pay off at thirty kilometers. I left Amsterdam the next morning with a belly full of cereal, bread, fruit, and chocolate, and while I sat on the train to Frankfurt watching the scenery pass by, I could almost hear the thousands and thousands of slow-twitch muscle fibers lapping up those carbos.

We arrived in Frankfurt a few days later and were greeted with all the hoopla that attends city marathons these days. Signs, banners, and posters announcing the First International Hoechst-Frankfurt Marathon were everywhere. Hoechst, Germany's enormous chemical company, is also the name of the Frankfurt suburb where much of the race takes place, and the company was determined that their sponsorship of Germany's largest marathon would also be a sponsorship of Germany's best marathon. Company personnel, and especially race director Hans Jurgensohn, had worked diligently for months to achieve that goal.

It's interesting to note the enthusiasm with which much of the world has taken to the marathon in recent years. It's no accident that many U.S. runners have suddenly been besieged with invitations to marathon races in cities that a few years ago would have considered the idea preposterous. Nearly every major city in Europe seems to have caught marathon fever. Amsterdam, Frankfurt, Rotterdam, Paris, and Antwerp in the spring. Stockholm, Oslo, and Helsinki in the late summer and fall. And I'm sure I've left a dozen others off the list. More established marathons through less congested areas of Europe are suffering from the popularity of liberating urban streets for a few hours of running. Somewhere behind this is the ethic of urban renewal. Frankfurt was no exception, and the city's enthusiasm over the thousands of participants in the event was contagious. I badly wanted to run well.

European runners do not typically celebrate before running, and thus the prerace spaghetti feed caught a lot of them off-stride.

"Wouldn't it be better to wait until after the race for all this?" one of the Irish runners wondered as the festivities began.

Still, the U.S.-style carbo-loading dinner went well, as race organizers introduced their field of invited runners from Great Britain, Greece, Canada, Egypt, Luxembourg, New Zealand, Spain, Portugal, Norway, Sweden, the Netherlands, the U.S., and Brazil. Thus did the specter of my Rio race haunt me as I sat down to the blandest meal I could assemble from the assorted pasta dishes on hand. There was no more room at the table with the U.S. flag on it, and I found myself sitting at one with the rising sun. And thus did the Tokyo race haunt my meal as well.

The next morning, during those few hours before the marathon when a runner considers all the things that can possibly go wrong in the twenty-six miles ahead, I reflected on some of the things that had destroyed other marathons I had run: dehydration, muscle fatigue, muscle tightness, groin pain, arch pain, knee pain, jet lag, blisters, sideaches, vomiting, and whatever combination of the above is called "hitting the wall." Though I had carbo loaded admirably this time, though I had avoided spicy foods, though my training had been good, and though the weather was reasonably cool on race day, I felt ill-at-ease. Rio and Tokyo were in the back of my mind, and there were still too many things that could go wrong.

When the gun fired, I began running what I hoped would be a conservative, solid race, far enough back in the field that the major problems would forget I was there, but close enough to the leaders that I would have a shot at the top few places.

The Frankfurt Marathon, as I've mentioned, was a well-organized affair. Precautions had been taken to ensure that runners were treated well before and during the marathon, that sufficient aid stations were available on the course, that spectators had been briefed about the top competitors in the race, and that times were accurately presented during and after the marathon. Each kilometer of the course was accurately measured and marked, which is why I can be sure of the precise point in the race where I stopped and began retching miserably.

It was at twenty-seven kilometers that nausea overcame me while I was struggling to stay in contact with two German runners who were traveling along in seventh or eighth place. It was right near the "27K" sign that my stomach began expressing its discontent at being attached to a body that had been shunting all its blood supply to its legs for the last hour-and-a-half. It was in the bushes next to the Main River that something green and unpleasant ended my hope of breaking out of a marathon slump. I threw up for ten minutes.

Farther along that same river, Kjell-Erik Stahl of Sweden was gradually breaking away from German favorite Gunter Mielke and Frank Richardson of the U.S., who had fallen victim to a sudden side stitch. Meanwhile, I was spitting green mucus and walking. Unable to find a ride, I finally began to jog slowly. Much, much later I finished.

I decided, during that first flash of emerald insight at the twenty-seven-kilometer mark, that I was through with marathons. One bad race in Rio was understandable. A second unpleasant clash with the wall in Tokyo was unsettling. But three strikes, as they say, and you're out. I was quitting marathons for good.

My mind was made up by the time I crossed the Schwanheimer Bridge and began the last few kilometers to the finish. I was hoping that Dan, who had been taking pictures from the press truck, would have the presence of mind to take a picture of me finishing my last marathon. Instead, he had the courtesy not to. I finished as discreetly as I could and headed for the showers.

For four days after the race, Dan and I spent time south of Frankfurt, in and around the city of Freiburg, while I recovered from the humiliation of my third disastrous marathon. Tom Steffens, a German runner, writer, and teacher I had met the previous fall, had volunteered to put us up for the remaining few days of our trip to Europe. During those days, while we enjoyed sightseeing and generous portions of Black Forest cake and German beer, I went on several easy runs through the woods, and my decision to give up the marathon became firmly fixed in my mind. When I mentioned it to Tom during discussions, he listened politely and then said, "Let's not talk about it now," or "You'll feel differently in a few days," or something else to indicate he was unwilling to accept the decision. When I mentioned it to Dan, he humored me by seeming to agree, knowing it wouldn't do any good to object anyway.

The beauty and serenity of the Black Forest made it a good place to consider the ramifications of the decision while nursing my body back to health, but by the time we were ready to head for home, my decision hadn't changed. I was glad to be free of the agonies of future marathons and anxious to pursue a different training program.

It's impossible to imagine any city that has been tortured, bled, and left to die with any greater success than Cleveland. The city's fate was sealed years ago, when the people with money decided to move to the suburbs. They were followed shortly afterward by the people without money, which has left Cleveland occupied only by people who are too burnt-out, cast-out, inebriated, or confused to care whether they have money or not. Long ago, the air was left to corrode, the lake to stagnate, and the river to burn, while millions of Ohioans stood conspicuously on the sidelines in embarrassment.

From the Black Forest, Dan and I traveled circuitously to Cleveland for the Road Runners Club of America National Convention and headed for a downtown hotel. Arrangements were soon made for us to run outside the city.

The area surrounding Cleveland turned out to be a stunning contrast to the city itself. During a long run with members of the Southeast Running Club, sponsors of the RRCA convention and part of the organizing team for the Revco-Cleveland Marathon and Ten-Kilometer Run, we trotted through some low-traffic rural areas a few miles outside of town whose beauty would be hard to surpass in any section of the country. But the very beauty of the scenery seemed to make our return to urban Cleveland even more depressing. Once I returned to the hotel, I didn't leave for almost two days.

In even the most devastated cities in the world there is generally a level of back-street energy, seedy activity, or downright viciousness within the city's core. Without being necessarily redeeming in nature, such areas at least pulsate with life. There seemed to be no such area in Cleveland. Instead, hopelessness echoed from the brick buildings, with only an assortment of derelicts on hand to hear the sound.

Nothing, though, is totally without hope. With unbounded and perhaps unwarranted faith in the future, prominent members of the Cleveland community joined the nationwide urban renewal campaign a few years ago, and since then pockets of rejuvenated Cleveland have evolved. A new building or two. A shopping arcade. A renovated hotel.

Somehow, the new life seems to confuse old-line bums. They sit numbly on benches and curbs downtown, waiting for the Final Curtain, and are as surprised at the rejuvenation campaign as they would be at a rich man stopping his Mercedes to ask if they'd like a ride to Shaker Heights. And they seemed just as confused to find thousands of runners lining up for a long-distance race through the city one Sunday morning in May.

One must admire the enthusiasm of Revco, race director Jack Staph, and the rest of the marathon organization for attempting to instill life into Cleveland with distance running. Somehow, after seeing what the city had to offer, it seemed like trying to cheer up a funeral by handing out smiley-face buttons. It seemed ludicrous to suggest that the footsteps of all those runners would be anything more than the ping-ping-ping of drops of water in the cellar of a deserted factory. The slogan "Bringing a City to Its Feet" was everywhere to promote the race, but the mood of the city, carried over to the race itself, was lethargic.

But then I wasn't in the best of moods. I was only a few days removed from my third disgusting marathon performance in a row, and I was going to be a difficult person to convince that a marathon of any sort would instill hope into a depressed entity.

I had given up the marathon, and I let people know it. Most thought I was kidding, or at least that my mood would pass. But I was happier with my decision each day and ecstatic not to be running another marathon that Sunday morning in Cleveland.

Both the marathon and the ten-kilometer run had attracted quality fields, with the shorter race in particular promising stellar competition among many of the world's top road racers. I stood at a point just short of the mile mark and the same distance from the finish on the out-and-back route, where I could get a good look at the race as it developed. In the park nearby, where spectators waited next to tramps for the runners to pass, a pigeon perched lazily on the head of the General Cleveland statue had the best view of all. Nearby, a small band was playing to generate excitement, but their music seemed to bounce off the buildings like the sound of a bee buzzing in an oil drum. This was not a scene compatible with energy. I was anxious to get this exercise in futility over with.

In a few minutes the gun fired and thousands of runners began their long trek. And then a miracle happened.

As I stood watching the first steps of all those runners, a spark ignited in the cobwebs in the back of my mind. A gentle magic began to work. As the racers passed at a five-minute clip, followed by an unfolding string of fun-runners, health-runners, age-group-runners, tall runners, small runners, fit runners, and fat runners, the strange beauty of this kind of event, where human beings of all persuasions test themselves against themselves and the road ahead, began to transform Cleveland into a city with some meager spirit.

It didn't last long. When the last of the pack passed, the buildings were there again, cold and impassive. A half-hour later, as the ten-kilometer runners went by, the city came alive again for a few minutes. And when Nick Rose swept past near the finish, followed by Thom Hunt, the sparks caught hold. I was getting wound up in this running thing.

I went back to my hotel room and sat down on the bed. I was moved by the ten-kilometer run, and that was fine. But what would the impending finish of the marathon do to my mind, after I had suffered thrice and made the monumental decision to quit the event? Was I going to follow through with the rational decision of someone who had endured three marathons of terrible consequence, or was I going to get caught up in the energy and mystique of the thing again?

Having asked the question, I returned to the street, walked to the finish line, and watched Charlie Vigil finish first for the second year in a row. As I watched, I tried to steel myself against the inevitable attraction that seemed to creep around the edges of my determination not to marathon again. I was partially successful.

That evening, Dan and I left Cleveland and headed back to Spokane. It was a long flight, offering a lot of time for thought. As we flew, I reflected on my trip, on my decision not to run marathons again, and on the way the marathon had helped transform a hopeless shell of a city into an area flickering with life, even if only for a few hours. Nothing, apparently, is beyond hope. Perhaps, I reasoned, I could find personal solace in that. Perhaps I shouldn't be so hasty in giving up the marathon. On the other hand, I had made my decision, and I was still pleased with the thought that I wouldn't have to shoot for twenty-six miles again. I would enter a new era, give up the familiarity of the marathon distance, begin anew. I promised myself that I wouldn't forget the dehydration, the blisters, the sideaches, the muscle cramps, the depletion, the throwing up at twenty-seven kilometers. I would honor the pledge to my body after all, and run no more marathons.

And then we stopped in Chicago, and a girl got on the plane and sat in the seat across the aisle. She had a teddy bear. Different girl this time, different teddy. If anything, this one was even sorrier than the one that had begun our trip. It was missing an eye, there were loose stitches in the side, and bare patches showed around the edges. It looked like it had run a marathon before boarding.

Agitated, I looked over at the poor thing. Sadder but wiser after all the trouble he'd obviously been through, he was still a comfort to the girl who cradled him in her lap as the plane took off, stroking his fur and soothing her fears.

"Dammit," I thought, "some people really don't know when it's time to move on."

Eye of the Tiger

> When your nose is bleeding and your eyes
> are black and you are so tired you wish your
> opponent would crack you on the jaw and
> put you to sleep, fight one more round re-
> membering that the man who fights one more
> round is never whipped.
>
> —GENTLEMAN JIM CORBETT

A COUPLE OF YEARS AGO I got into a discussion with another auto-mobile driver over proper traffic flow. Two shots to my face and he won the argument, giving me a lesson in humility and the left hook. For weeks my face swelled with evidence of what it's like to earn one's living as a prizefighter.

The marathon can teach similar lessons. It can hit hard, quickly, and ruthlessly, and only a fool attempts to battle it without adequate preparation. Naturally, every marathon has more than its fair share of fools.

A day after the 1981 Honolulu Marathon, I was running five miles with Boston radio and television commentator Tony Reavis. I had watched the race the previous day from the lead vehicle, calling in reports to Reavis for KKUA radio every mile or so, watching Jon Anderson maintain his margin of victory over Duncan Macdonald. Macdonald, in turn, was almost nipped in the last few meters by a hard-charging Kjell-Erik Stahl of Sweden. As Reavis and I ran the next afternoon, we spoke in particular of Stahl, who seems to thrive on repeated marathon racing. The Hawaii race was reported to be his eleventh of the year. A week earlier he had finished twelfth at Fukuoka, only to return to the marathon at Honolulu, where he led the field for fourteen miles before finally finishing third behind Mac-donald.

"That guy is unbelievable," said Reavis. "I was out this morning and saw him running again, the day after the marathon!"

"I saw him, too," I said. We compared notes, and it appeared that Stahl had either been running for over an hour that morning or else had had two separate morning runs. As we marveled at his swift return to training after a hard marathon effort, amazed and amused at his resiliency, we spotted him again.

There, heading back toward Waikiki on either his second or third training run the day after a 2:17 marathon, went Kjell-Erik Stahl, already preparing himself for his next go-round with the twenty-six-miler.

Stahl is not the fool mentioned earlier. Rather, his hollow cheeks and generally somber disposition suggest Edvard Munch's famous painting *The Scream*. In Stahl's case, though, the figure in the painting might well be howling, "The Tokyo Marathon in two weeks? Nooooooo!"

And yet Stahl seems to take to his task without fear, superbly prepared, ready to go one more round with the champion, the marathon. Never whipped.

Not all of us are so fortunate. In the past few years, marathoning has spiraled worse than inflation. While the growth of road racing in the U.S. has centered on the ten-kilometer distance, the phenomenon elsewhere has found its expression in the marathon. Virtually every major city around the world now has a "major" marathon, and the attraction of the event has led many of us to try it too often. Stahl, at least, seems prepared for the onslaught. Many of us end up flat on our backs.

My last full marathon attempt was in Frankfurt, Germany, on May 17, 1981. After that race, in which I started with high hopes and fell apart—broken, vomiting, depressed—at just under thirty kilometers, I swore off marathons. There had been two prior disasters at the distance, and the third strike meant I was out. Knocked out, perhaps.

The winner of that Frankfurt race, incidentally, was a tall, thin, dour, and determined-looking Swede named Kjell-Erik Stahl.

By the time of the 1981 Honolulu Marathon, I was already questioning my decision to give up marathons. As Reavis and I ran, I was contemplating a return to the Islands a year later as a competitor, not a radio commentator. The Honolulu Marathon would be celebrating its tenth anniversary, they would be inviting back all past winners, and it seemed as good a time as any to jump back into the ring. I'm not sure why the boxing metaphor seems so appropriate to the nonviolent sport of running. Certainly the personal aspect of long-distance running, where success rests with the individual rather than the team, is similar to boxing. Perhaps the violence of boxing, directed at another individual, is sublimated in running, becoming a different kind of aggression. Both sports definitely require coming to terms with personal suffering in pursuit of success. But more than anything, it is the long hours of preparation that link boxing and running. And both sports, consequently, require a particularly personal honesty, the absence of which is extremely painful.

When Muhammed Ali got into the ring with Larry Holmes for his fourth try at the world championship two years ago, the world took a deep breath. The man was too old, too slow, too heavy. And yet this was Muhammed Ali, who could work magic. A few rounds into the match, though, when the boxer's magic failed to materialize, the world looked the other way. Unprepared for the encounter, Ali was pummeled repeatedly, paying a painful price. Mercifully, the ex-champ wasn't forced to go the distance.

For my own part, I had become convinced that my last three marathons had exacted a painful toll primarily because I wasn't ready for them. Before going the distance again, I would get ready. Play the theme from *Rocky*, please.

Anyone who has made a marathon comeback, from illness, an injury, or a layoff, knows the feeling. Days of sluggishness, when lazy muscles are asked to be active again. Weeks of gradual increases, when a ten-mile run is ultradistance and a twenty-miler impossible. Months of planning, when the long-term goal seems a fuzzy dream, too near to prepare for or too distant to be relevant.

And moments of despair, when the time and effort spent seem out of proportion to the projected rewards.

At the low ebb of my training slump, I was running twenty miles a week. Slowly. In a way, the slump was enjoyable. Injuries receded. Energy increased. I accomplished large amounts of work during the day, and I ate dinner at dinner time. I read books again, and discovered television. My weight ballooned up to 155 pounds. My wife Bridgid told me it was nice having me around again.

As a result, when I began increasing my training, the long road back seemed even longer. What might have taken me six weeks to accomplish at age twenty was now taking twelve weeks or more. With other commitments impending, it seemed frivolous to be spending so much time preparing for the marathon, and my training suffered as a result. I got injured easier and recovered slower. The fatigue of a hard workout lasted for days.

My original rationale for giving up the marathon had been solid. The event is generally overrated, tending to overshadow shorter races. The time required to prepare and recover from it drains energy that might otherwise be used for 10K races, track events, cross-country, and of course nonrunning activities. The risk of injury is high and the chance of hitting some sort of wall is excellent.

But in spite of all this I had decided to go at least one more round with the marathon, for whatever reason, and slowly but surely I made progress. Seventy miles a week became comfortable. Morning workouts were added. Nagging pains in my legs diminished, and I began twenty-mile runs again. I had decided to include quality work—intervals, hill repeats, fartlek—from the very beginning, rather than concentrating on increased mileage alone. The plan was successful, and my leg-speed improved along with my endurance. Once again, though, what had been swift progress at age twenty in terms of speed was now, at age thirty-three, painfully slow.

In the best of times intervals are no fun. During a comeback they're acutely miserable. Facing a set of ten hills one evening, standing in the dark at the bottom of a quarter-mile slope, I experienced the mild despair that seems to precede any interval workout. Stretching my hamstrings, calves, quadriceps, and groin in anticipation of the repeated anaerobic pain ahead, I tried to focus on Apollo Creed's words to Rocky Balboa.

With genuine inspiration and considerable amusement, I began the evening's workout repeating the words that would become my comeback theme.

"Eye of the tiger, Rocky. Eye of the tiger."

I was not alone in arriving in Honolulu ready to make a comeback of sorts. The comeback theme is a consistent one for this marathon, with the general thought process seeming to end with the line, ". . . and if I don't do well, at least I'll be in Hawaii to recover."

The 1982 Honolulu Marathon would be Frank Shorter's fourth Hawaiian comeback attempt in as many years, following a frustrating pattern of injury, recovery, reinjury, surgery, and recovery that had finally brought Frank back to road-race form but not marathon success. Kenny Moore made a marathon comeback attempt at Honolulu in 1978, finishing with a 2:19:09 performance, and gave up serious marathoning shortly thereafter.

Jack Foster, winner of the 1975 race at the age of forty-three, now retired from active marathoning and running only three times a week, was in town for a 1982 comeback of modest expectations.

Duncan Macdonald, hometown boy and three-time Honolulu winner, had come back again to the Islands for his yearly marathon attempt. Or perhaps biyearly, since a 2:13 performance earlier in the year at Chicago had made him the 1982 Honolulu favorite, along with returning champion Jon Anderson.

And, of course, Kjell-Erik Stahl was in town for his thirteenth comeback of 1982. Miami, Beppu, Rome, Boston, Rotterdam, Stockholm, Örebro, Rio de Janeiro, Athens, Chicago, Columbus, New York, and now Honolulu.

The days leading up to Sunday's event were unusually festive, even for Honolulu, a marathon known for its love of celebrating before, during, and after the actual footracing. As part of the marathon's ten-year anniversary, officials had organized a seven-day agenda of festivities. More than ten thousand entrants were on hand to enjoy a week of dining, dancing, and dashing around Waikiki, leaving little time for worrying about the twenty-six miles ahead.

When they weren't joining in the celebrations, the few reporters and others interested in picking a winner of Sunday's race cruised among the athletes, looking for inside information on who was fit and who wasn't. The smart money seemed to rest on Macdonald and Anderson, with Shorter a serious outside shot and Stahl a possibility. Tony Reavis, though, back in town to commentate for KKUA radio, jokingly suggested that Stahl, with a five-week hiatus from marathoning, had had too much rest this year and wouldn't be a factor.

I was asked a number of times about my own level of fitness. I answered honestly that I was making a marathon comeback, hoping for a modest 2:20 effort, and planning for a full effort in mid-January at the Houston-Tenneco Marathon. Reporters are used to hearing runners downplay their own fitness, speak with awe of other runners in the field, and then go on to win the race, so there was some reluctance to take me at my word.

Jim Barahal, a local runner and physician known as Dr. Sport on radio, was especially keen on seeing me pull an upset. But I had enough of a sense of my current condition to know that the likelihood of an upset was low.

"This is just going to be a 2:20 effort for me," I told him again. "If you're looking for a dark horse, go with Dave Gordon."

"Dave who?" he asked, smiling.

"Dave Gordon. He's a young runner from Olympia, Washington. Went to college in Montana."

"What's he done?"

"He's been running well in the Northwest," I said. "He was third at Bloomsday in Spokane, and he's run a couple of great races in the Seattle area."

Barahal hesitated. "What do you think about Shorter?" he finally asked.

In fact, though, Dave Gordon was a good bet to surprise a few people. Young and eager to prove himself in the Honolulu field of veterans, he had enjoyed 1982 as a breakthrough year, running head-to-head with the likes of Rodgers, Shorter, Lindsay, Rono, and Sinclair. He is only a notch, and a slim notch at that, from the very top, and he runs aggressively and fearlessly. At Honolulu, he might

suffer the fate of a couple of other young runners in past years—
Tom Wysocki and Jon Sinclair—who raced well early before run-
ning into trouble around twenty miles. Or, like 1979 winner Dean
Matthews, he might fool the veterans and steal the marbles.

I saw Barahal again on Saturday morning, the day before the
race.

"How're you feeling?" he asked.

"I feel good, Jim," I answered, but he was asking more than
that, still suspecting I might be preparing an upset.

"You really look fit this year," he said. "Last year you seemed
kind of heavy. You were clearly out of shape. But you look real thin
this year."

"I got a haircut," I said. "People always tell me I've lost weight
when I get a haircut."

"You're still planning to run a 2:20?"

"I'm going out at 2:20 pace," I answered. "If I feel great I'll pick
it up. But I really don't want to go a hundred percent here. My goal
is still Houston."

Barahal continued to fish for a winner. "It seems like most people
here are picking Duncan," he said. "What do you think?"

"Duncan's in great shape," I answered. "He'll be tough to beat.
But I still think Dave Gordon's got a good chance."

"I don't know," Barahal said. "I talked with him yesterday. I
don't think he's ready to win. He didn't look like he wanted it that
bad."

"Maybe not," I answered, and the conversation turned to other
things.

That evening I ate dinner with a few friends, Macdonald included. In my first Honolulu Marathon in 1976 Duncan had taken
me to a Mexican restaurant for a prerace dinner. The next morning
I threw up at nineteen miles and Duncan won the race. Since then
I've been superstitious about prerace meals. Two out of my last
three races had seen me throwing up before the finish, and I didn't
want it to be three for four after the next day's race. The evening
before my 1978 Honolulu victory I had had chicken, so this time I
had it again, and then headed back to the hotel for bed.

The Honolulu Marathon starts at 6:00 A.M., so an early bedtime is advisable. I had just drifted off to sleep when the phone rang.

"Don?" It was Barahal. "Hey, I'm sorry to bother you, but I wanted to ask you again what some of Dave Gordon's best performances are."

I mentioned a couple.

"Okay, thanks," he said. "I'm going to go ahead and pick him on the radio tomorrow as a favorite. But I couldn't remember any of his performances. Thanks a lot. Good luck tomorrow."

Dave Gordon. Eye of the tiger. I fell asleep.

The Honolulu Marathon is not without its niceties, but the early starting time is not one of them. At 4:30 A.M. the hotel operator called. By 6:00 A.M. I had joined ten thousand other runners on the starting line.

A light rain had fallen earlier, raising the humidity but not lowering the temperature much. When the cannon blew, we were all off to a hot, muggy start.

The first few miles of the Honolulu Marathon are run in the dark, and as a result I missed seeing the first mile marker. I spotted the two-mile mark, though, and realized that at 10:40 I was right on projected pace: 5:20 per mile, 2:20 marathon effort.

While I muddled around with my modest goals, Frank Shorter was on kamikaze pace: 4:54 at the mile, 9:58 at two miles, and well in the lead. In a different race, Frank's pace of under five minutes per mile wouldn't have seemed extreme. At Honolulu, where times are generally four minutes slower than elsewhere, his pace left a lot of fast runners behind.

In retrospect, Frank's plan seemed to be to go out at five-minute pace, hoping he could maintain a lead and steal the race. In reality there were at least three quick runners, Macdonald, Stahl, and Gordon, breathing down his neck. By ten miles Stahl and Gordon had reeled Frank in. It was becoming a duel between the perennial marathoner, Stahl, and the newcomer, the challenger, Dave Gordon.

My own perspective on the race was, of course, much different. I worked to stay relaxed at 5:20 per mile, hearing as I passed the five-mile mark that Shorter was leading, and wondering whether the old champ's comeback would be successful.

As I passed the same ten-mile point where Gordon and Stahl had caught Shorter, I noted the time and realized I was still on pace. I had passed aid stations to avoid stomach problems, I had maintained a steady pace, and I was feeling good. Then the weather changed.

The newspaper described it the next day as a mini–Hurricane Iwa, the storm that had ravished the Islands a few weeks earlier. From my perspective, it was a twenty-minute fistfight with the elements, as sheets of wind and rain blew across the course. My legs tightened, my stomach cramped, and fancy footwork became a necessity in traveling down the flooded street. Marathon volunteers huddled under umbrellas and tarps to stay dry, and aid-station sponges were used to dry off rather than get wet.

It seemed as if the storm might last for the rest of the race, but just as suddenly as it had started, it stopped.

A spectator held out towels as if, clairvoyant, he had anticipated the storm and planned accordingly. I found myself running next to Boulder runner Stan Mavis, who, similarly clairvoyant, had worn a baseball cap to keep the rain out of his eyes. Mavis and I broke through the storm at fourteen miles, both, I think, suffering from the experience.

And of course we were not alone. Up front, Shorter had headed to the side of the road for a pit stop just as the storm (and Stahl and Gordon) reached him. From my vantage point farther back, I suddenly spotted Frank running about a hundred yards ahead of me, and I tried to take my mind off the growing fatigue by keying my strategy for the next few miles on catching him.

Meanwhile, Gordon and Stahl ran together through fair weather and foul until just past fourteen miles, when the younger runner made his move. By fifteen miles he had a lead, and from there to the finish he continued to lengthen it, feeling strong until twenty miles, but continuing to lengthen his margin even as he tired near the end. Gordon finished in 2:15:29, over a minute better than the course record, enormously pleased with his marathon breakthrough. Eye of the tiger.

A little farther back, Duncan Macdonald caught Kjell-Erik Stahl to take second, both runners turning in times nearly identical to last year's.

Much farther back, I struggled to stay with Mavis, who seemed to move up easily to catch and pass Shorter at about seventeen miles. Eventually I couldn't see him anymore. A Japanese runner, Katsuhiro Tachikawa, passed me a little later and went after Shorter. Mavis passed me again. He had made a pit stop of his own.

By twenty miles I had almost caught Shorter, but from that point on Frank moved away, eventually taking fifth place, behind Tachikawa, in 2:22:16. Shorter was followed by John Gailson (2:22:39), Mavis (2:22:56), Jon Anderson (2:23:11), and, in ninth place, inordinately pleased with completing twenty-six miles in a time of 2:23:28 without breaking down, throwing up, or dropping out, me.

The last six miles had held a fair amount of fatigue, nausea, and suffering, but I had made it to the finish line on my feet. I had gone the distance. Let's hear that theme from *Rocky*, please, one more time. With feeling.

Shortly after finishing, as my wife Bridgid and I wandered through the picnic area at Kapiolani Park, I spotted Jim Barahal, radio's Dr. Sport, once again.

"Hey, thanks for the tip on Gordon," he said. "I owe you one."

I hadn't been the only one to mention Gordon to Barahal. Bridgid had been even more emphatic about Gordon's abilities, and her sentiments had been echoed by others as Barahal had painstakingly done his prerace interviewing. As a result, he had gone on the air early that morning to name Gordon as a prerace favorite. No one else in town had heard of him.

The long-shot choice had been impressive. It was like picking Leon Spinks over Muhammed Ali a few years back. Dr. Sport had done his job well.

Barahal left, and Bridgid and I walked to the start of the homestretch of the marathon. As hundreds upon hundreds of runners passed by in varying degrees of elation and exhaustion, I wondered what marathon stories they might be completing themselves. In all likelihood, in fact, this tenth Honolulu Marathon, with over ten thousand stories to tell, was also telling the story of its own future.

In years to come, the Honolulu race would undoubtedly continue to follow its course as a self-proclaimed "people's race," catering to thousands of runners from Hawaii and the mainland who want to celebrate their marathon attempts in Honolulu, with fireworks at the start, Tahitian dancers at nine miles, enthusiastic volunteers and spectators throughout the race, and a shell necklace at the finish line. Oh, yes, and possibly a midrace hurricane.

In another respect, it would also continue to produce competition between young runners on their way up in the world of marathoning, the Dave Gordons of the sport, and older runners, who have generally seen better marathoning days.

The middle group of competitive runners, the prime candidates for heavyweight champion of the marathoning world, will probably save their races for other courses, where greater prestige and money abound.

My own story had ended happily that day. The 2:23:28 was a fair distance from my personal best of 2:11:16. Miles, in fact. In light of my recent marathon performances, though, the ones that drove me to quit, I was immensely satisfied. With a marathon of 2:23 under my belt, I could begin thinking about 2:18 and below. I could contemplate a fast race in Houston a few weeks later.

Measured against Gordon's 2:15:29, of course, a time worth 2:11 under more favorable conditions, 2:23 didn't seem like much. It was difficult to avoid feeling a certain amount of envy for Gordon, a young runner on the brink of his best competitive years.

And yet finally, when all was said and done, the 2:23 set well. Unlike Muhammed Ali, those of us in the marathon fight choose our own opponents—2:10, 2:20, three hours, or just going the distance. All we have to do is choose wisely, jump back into the ring, and fight the good fight.

And those of us inclined to envy the Dave Gordons of the sport can still take heart from the thirty-six-year-old Swede Kjell-Erik Stahl, who had finished third that day, and who would most certainly be out training again the next day, already preparing himself for yet another bout with the twenty-six-miler.

Eye of the tiger indeed.

1980 OLYMPIC DIARY

I think we Americans may be world champions at forgetting the past. Certainly we're world class. In directing the fate of our nation, we've felt relatively unburdened by history, and when past mistakes are mentioned, someone is always ready to chime in with, "Well, let's not dwell on that." Perhaps this is a virtue.

History does teach lessons, though, and one would hope that there are lessons to be learned from the collapse of the Olympic aspirations of thousands of athletes, American and other, who were training for the 1980 Olympics when President Carter put the boycott wheels in motion. This "Olympic Diary" series reflects that experience as seen through one set of eyes and considered by one intellect.

I began writing this group of articles at the invitation of *Running Times* editor Ed Ayres. The initial articles represent an attempt, mostly humorous and anecdotal, to explain what it's like to nurture an Olympic dream: to plan, to hope, to remember, and to experience the daily frustrations en route to fulfillment.

As it turned out, though, the series became a record of a quest that was short-circuited. When I reread the last few articles, I see myself groping for meaning, trying to come to terms with a questionable political decision. The lesson the aborted Olympics taught was—what? Detachment from aspirations? Caution? Cynicism?

I hope not. There is little room for emotional caution in an Olympic bid. One must believe, ignoring Murphy's law.

I think the lesson of the 1980 Olympics is a seasonal one. Things get worse. Things get better. Dreams die. New dreams are born.

People have talked a lot about "the Olympic ideal" in the past few years, though it's not always apparent what they're referring to. To my mind, the ideal is clear: high-spirited competition among the best athletes in the world, irrespective of race, creed, color, national origin, or shoe size. The pure drive of human effort, fueled by human dreams. An ideal worth preserving, no matter who seeks to pervert it. An ideal that very often seems to be sheltered only in the hearts of those who strive to be part of it.

You may be thinking "Let's not dwell on that" yourself. Why worry about 1980? Didn't the 1984 Games in Los Angeles suggest that things are all better for idealism and international sport?

Americans have been led to believe so, and there were certainly areas in which the 1984 Games were brilliant and inspirational, suggesting that the ideal is alive and well. But don't tell that to any of the thousands of athletes who had to stay home. In 1984, politics once again took a nasty bite out of Olympic competiton.

When all was said and done, though, most observers still gave L.A. a decent score. And if L.A. represented a warming trend in recent Olympic history, in spite of the repeated intrusion of politics, perhaps spring is on the way for the Games. If so, we might expect the world to begin allowing athleticism its few minutes of unimpeded, joyous expression every four years. The events of 1980, then, which are reported here by one observer, when politics stifled the spirit of thousands of athletes, should remind us of what it is we want to avoid.

At the time, 1980 seemed to mark the dead of winter for the Olympic ideal, and the last few articles in this series reflect that sense. But as the bard once said, "If winter comes, can spring be far behind?"

(JULY 1979)

The Crab Toilet Omen

"Too much . . . too much," I mumbled in the slang I've never been able to outgrow.

"Too much money? Or just too much?" asked the salesperson.

About fifty years old, the lady was trying to sift through my mumblings, sniffing out a potential sale. She had surprised me.

"Uh . . . just . . . too much," I returned. I was in the presence of some kind of omen, I knew, and I resented her mercantile intrusion.

In front of me was an object of startling implications. A possible signpost to the future or symbol, perhaps, of the past. I knew, I knew there was a lesson to be learned here in this souvenir shop on Route 101. One recognizes objects of importance, and senses vortices of meaning, even as the importance and meaning hide behind the object's skirts like embarrassed children.

I stared at the toilet seat, awestruck.

A toilet seat made almost entirely of acrylic, an acrylic that encased perhaps a hundred small crabs (the decapod crustaceans of littoral note, not the licentious parasites of the Anoplura order). I was looking at a crab toilet seat.

Someone had created this lowbrow physical pun and put it up for sale for his own reasons, but I stood transfixed, sensing enlightenment for my own reasons.

Such signs are not easily read.

After several unenlightened moments, I gave up and made my way out the door. Outside, I walked past a man who had his chainsaw stuck in the eye of a wooden Indian, doing the last delicate touch-up work on his carving. This might have caught me as another omen, but I was still absorbed with the crab toilet seat. I climbed into my van and headed back down the Oregon coast.

I was recovering from a devastating defeat at Portland's Cascade Run-Off. Last year, after running the marathon in Athens, traveling through Greece for a month, and flying for nineteen hours to get back to Portland in time, I had run 45:48 for the fifteen-kilometer race. This year I came into the race well-rested and well-prepared, and ran 47:22. I went immediately into the kind of depression that needs a lot of running to get through.

My running career had been punctuated with this type of humiliating turn of the logical order. I'm a manic-depressive runner, with tremendous highs and unforgiving lows. There have been a string of blessed, glorious performances like my Olympic experience and a string of damnable races that defy my ability to understand them.

Bill Rodgers amazes me. I'm not surprised at his ability to run 2:10 for the marathon and to whip the best runners in the world at shorter distances. That makes sense. What amazes me is his consistency. His unabashed consistency.

Like any other manic-depressive marveling at how some people sail smoothly, I wonder at Bill's stability at the front of the pack. At Boston last spring I watched him leading a group of twenty contenders to the Prudential like a bull goose guiding his wedge of Canadian honkers. Bill, as usual, was the first to arrive.

I want no lithium cure for my manic-depressive running. I don't want consistency at the expense of the highs. I'll accept the lows when they're where they should be: in the off-season, after a hard training session, and so on. What I'm struggling with is predictability. As I cruise into another Olympic year, I'd like to put my performance peaks where they should be: at the Olympic Trials and the Olympic Games.

Can a crab toilet seat help?

Driving and running, driving and running, I continued to search for meaning in my poor showing in Portland.

Perhaps, I surmised, as I ran into a sadistic head wind one morning, I should do more simulation of the conditions to expect at Buffalo at the Olympic Marathon Trials. They have frequent head winds. Should I do this more often?

Or, urging my VW bus up one of a series of camel-hump hills another morning, I considered that I might be neglecting hill work in my training. I've got to work it in somewhere, right?

But then I can't forget the long runs, can I? This brilliant thought hung with me during a short afternoon run that seemed infinite.

Altitude? Is that the key? Mile-high Crater Lake offered no answer to the altitude question it presented. But wouldn't it help, really?

Days of rumination passed. The answer, the secret, was somewhere. I kept thinking, thinking, thinking.

We do that, don't we? We run day after day, thinking over the same events, the same problems, the same dreams. We are hack philosophers who seem to thrive on nothing so much as the chumminess of familiar thoughts during our runs. I have asked myself these same training questions before. I know the answers, generally. And yet the problem of putting all the answers into a training package that will put me into the Olympic Games again is eluding me.

On a clear, warm morning near Bend, Oregon, I ran along country roads with only slight muscular pain, the fading remnants of my debacle in Portland flickering in my legs. The air was still, heavy with the aroma of pine trees baking in the sun. A few grasshoppers were clicking loudly, but their noise only increased the sense of overwhelming stillness.

The image of the crab toilet seat came to mind again, but this time I smiled, because suddenly it made sense.

Above all else, I realized, there has been this overwhelming, constant flirtation with daydreaming in my life. Running has provided the time and place for it to take place, and I've spent hours entertained by my own thoughts on the run. Running has been the pusher for my junkie mind. I daily crave the fix, although the fix fixes nothing. I am addicted to long, slow thinking.

The crab toilet seat is the key. Who could daydream sitting on it? It says what I needed to hear: "Sit no more, thinking. Get up. Act!" Perhaps this, more than anything, was what the toilet seat's creator (Dare I say "artist"?) was trying to say: "Ahoy, there! Get up and get going, lad, you've got crabs on your rear and you can't sit there all day, dreaming."

I made a decision that day. I decided to do something about my training. I made up my mind to call my coach when I got back to Spokane, to implement a plan of action for Moscow 1980. Together we'll transform those scattered ideas on training, inconsistency, and peaking into a definite training schedule. And I'll follow it, a reformed man.

I owe it all to that crab toilet seat.

Too much, indeed. At only ninety-five dollars, I should never have left the damn thing sitting there in the shop. Even now, I imagine some meathead yokel gawking at my life's oracle and saying, "Hey, Madge, will you look at this. A toilet seat with crabs. Ha ha ha ha ha ha . . ."

(AUGUST 1979)

Elvis, Gnats, Etc.

ABOUT TWO MONTHS AGO I attended a wedding I won't soon forget. For one thing, I won't forget trying to survive a Catholic mass when my legs had been previously flagellated with thirty miles of running. Hamstrings, quads, and calf muscles joined with the priest in urging me to kneel in prayer for the bride and groom.

Afterward I wandered to the reception with my friend Bridgid, who gave brief biographical sketches of the invited guests. Although most of the people were initially unknown to me, Bridgid helped construct a web of habits, quirks, idiosyncrasies, and interrelationships that eventually imposed meaning on the assembled throng.

Sometime during the afternoon she singled out a dark-haired man in his late twenties, nicely dressed in a three-piece suit, who was talking with the bride's younger sister.

"That's Bill Martino," said Bridgid. "He was heavy into Elvis when we were in grade school."

"What do you mean?" I asked. "He was a big fan of Elvis, or what?"

"He practiced Elvis songs all the time. He was nuts for Elvis. He used to call my friend Julie in seventh grade and sing 'Hound Dog,' 'Jail House Rock,' and all that other Elvis stuff for her. She couldn't believe it."

I looked back at the culprit. He was dancing with the bride's sister as she soared champagne-wise. Fourteen years old, she would regret her intemperance later, but in the meantime Bill Martino was playing the role of big brother. As the band played modest rock music, Bill guided his young partner away from expensive furnishings and gray-haired relatives as best he could.

As I watched the two on the dance floor, Bridgid finalized her explanation. "Let me put it this way. When the girls were playing horsies and the boys were playing army, Bill was playing Elvis."

Hard to believe, I thought. The guy had obviously come quite a long way from his Elvis days, looking dapper, successful, and mature on this sunny afternoon.

During a lull in the music, the lead singer made a sudden announcement. "We have a special request," he intoned. "We have someone who'd like to sing a song for the bride and groom."

Bill Martino stepped confidently to the microphone. He snapped a signal to the band, and the drums and guitars began hammering out the rhythm. And the King sang.

"You know I can be found/Sitting home all alone/If you can't come around/At least please telephone/Don't be cruel/To a heart that's true."

I looked at Bridgid. Her chin dropped, then she smiled. "I don't believe this," she whispered. "I don't believe he's still doing this."

He was. And very well, too, embellishing the lyrics with appropriate Elvis body movements. We both stared for several minutes in delighted wonder as the King wound up his performance.

"I don't want no other love/Baby, it's just you I'm dreaming of."

The King gave a final signal to the band, and they ended on cue. Polite clapping from the adults, raucous whooping from the younger guests. Bill Martino, the King, had made his mark.

A few days later I was sitting in the El Rio Cafe, talking with Ed Schaefer, the proprietor. Ed controls his naturally weighty bulk with a few miles of running several times a week. He also serves some of the best Mexican food in town.

"When's your next big race?" he asked as he set a hot burrito-enchilada dinner on the table.

"The Nike Marathon," I answered. "On September ninth. Hopefully I'll get my Olympic Trials qualifying time there."

"Oh, you're going for another Olympics, eh?"

"Yeah, one more."

"What are your chances?"

"Well," I began, covering familiar territory, "if I get my qualifying time at Nike, I'll be running the Trials next May in Buffalo. If I'm in the top three there I'm on the team. It sounds simple, doesn't it?"

Ed laughed. "I guess so. Anyway, best of luck to you."

I looked out the window to where dozens of tiny bugs were circling a spotlight. They danced around in tight circles in the light for no obvious reason, following some bizarre urging. As they did so, they traced out patterns of light that were almost decipherable, the way we used to do with sparklers on the Fourth of July, spelling messages to each other.

Ten years ago, when I was in college, there would surely have been someone nearby who, with the help of some available psychedelic substance, could have interpreted the erratic tracings of those bugs. Now, with only a couple of Budweisers to my credit, I was mesmerized without being enlightened. I was considering my Olympic chances.

The speed of marathon running has not changed much since I made my leap to the Olympic team in 1976. The world record still belongs to Derek Clayton. Bill Rodgers '79 would have beaten Bill Rodgers '75 by about a block over the Boston course. A pittance.

With four years under my belt, my chances of making the team would seem to be better than ever. My strength has improved as my mileage has increased. I've studied and experimented with different pacing strategies, different training methods, and different diets, so my knowledge of marathon artistry has sharpened. I've even reformed from LSD addiction and am rebuilding my speed, thanks to the renaissance of coaching in my workout scheme.

In a nutshell, I've been practicing this song for quite a few years now, and I ought to just about have it right. Like Bill Martino, I've been practicing for the big moment and am hoping the rhythm, tempo, and melody add up to a spot on the hit parade.

And what about those bugs outside the El Rio window? They circled and circled the light, enthralled, in some kind of insect ritual. It isn't hard, by God, to imagine yourself running quarter-mile intervals on the track when you're staring at a bunch of light-inebriated gnats.

The scene held no peace for my Olympics-captivated skull. I realized that the skies are clouded these days with excellent marathon runners, dozens of whom can nail down a spot on the Olympic team on the right day.

So many newborn marathoners—training, training, training. Practicing their songs and dreaming of a spot on the hit parade. The thought made me feel very vulnerable.

As the bugs circled the spotlight, I suddenly noticed that things were happening to upset the cyclical stability of the scene. One swirled too close to the light and—ZAP!—burned out, falling in a neat plumb line to the pavement. Another seemed to circle too quickly and—BING!—flew off erratically into the darkness as if injured.

It happened over and over again, some buzzing out of view and some heading down in gnat nosedives. For no clear reason, some survived and some didn't. Eventually, I thought, there'll only be a few left.

I stared captivated by this kind of nonsense until Ed's voice startled me. "Closing up," he said.

"Oh, yeah . . . okay." I got up, paid the bill, and headed for the door. On my way out, I took another look at the gnat galaxy. I'm there somewhere, I thought. And to whomever was currently deciding gnat fates, I sent out the message: "Don't be cruel/To a heart that's true."

"Good night, Ed."

"Good night," he said closing the door behind me. "Good luck with your running."

President Carter's Running Mate

WHEN I got the invitation to run with President Carter, my mind began wheeling deviously. I'm a glutton for certain types of publicity, and though I'm not quick enough or funny enough to be a stand-up comedian, I do know the value of a situation, and I know where the reporters and photographers will be.

I determined, well in advance, the line that would make national TV, putting my face on the six o'clock news.

Imagine this: The President of the United States is on the awards platform, handing me my award. I shake his hand, step to the mike, pause, and say, "A lot of people have asked me during the past few weeks whether I was worried about losing this race to President Carter. . . ." Pause again. Let the words settle on the crowd. "And I told them all the same thing. . . ." Final pause. "I don't care if I beat President Carter or not, but if Kennedy runs I'll whip his ass!"

The line struck me, in my imagination, like the discovery of universal gravitation or the structure of the benzene molecule. Big, Big Stuff.

Years ago I was approached by Tom Jordan of *Track and Field News*, who wanted to know to what I attributed the dramatic improvement of my three-mile time. "I owe it all to my diet," I told him, paraphrasing a ridiculous article I had once read.

"Oh?" Tom responded, expectantly. "So what's your diet been like?"

I seem to remember a tingle in my backbone as I answered, "Froot Loops for breakfast, peanut butter and jelly sandwiches and a bag of cookies for lunch, beer and pizza for dinner." An accurate answer, one that he scribbled down, one that I knew, in a rare, transcendent moment, would follow me stride for stride through the rest of my athletic career.

I knew, when the lines first came to me, that whipping Kennedy's ass had the same comedic charisma. It would make the news. A slightly disrespectful but basically good-natured line with political overtones could not miss. I had a winner.

Some people think I don't take this Olympic Games shindig very seriously. That's not true.

Even as I was imagining myself hobnobbing with President Carter and making the national news, I was in serious training for the Nike Marathon. It was to be my qualifying race for the Olympic Trials, my first step to Moscow, the culmination of a summer of fairly rigorous training. It was also a week before the run with Jimmy.

During the summer, the essential marathon question that burned its mark in my ruminations was: Should I go for the win, or run to qualify? The Nike Marathon promised to be fast and competitive, and I lusted after a quality performance. On the other hand, not having qualified for the Olympic Trials, the logical approach was to run conservatively, avoiding the blow-ups that often occur in going for broke over twenty-six miles.

Two views of the Honolulu Marathon, seen through my eyes, represented two sides of the question. Nineteen seventy-eight: the glorious glow of strength and emotion I felt as I surged down the final quarter-mile past rows of screaming spectators. Victory. Nineteen seventy-six: throbbing head, blurred vision, weak legs, and a stomach pumping up something unwanted at twenty miles. Defeat.

I needed that qualifying time. I was already leaning toward conservatism when the final argument crept into the courtroom and presented itself. President Carter would not be giving any award in front of any national news media to any marathon runner who finished out of the money in a ten-kilometer race, no matter how fast he could run twenty-six miles.

The Nike Marathon would be September ninth. The Catoctin Mountain National Park Ten-Kilometer, featuring Jimmy Carter, was a week later. If I ran the marathon conservatively on the ninth, I might make the victory stand on the fifteenth. Then I could be funny and famous.

Nobody was committing himself. I sat with some of the *Running Times* staff at the prerace spaghetti feed, and they kept asking me if Carter was going to show up for dinner. How would I know, I wondered, when the people who really should have known were saying, "Maybe," or "He said he might," or "He's just down the road at Camp David," or whatever.

He didn't show. I went to bed.

The whole weekend was like that. Like a group of UFO aficionados who had received telepathic notice of an impending arrival, we waited expectantly. But even as race time approached, there seemed to be no guarantee from anyone that the president would be there. Didn't they realize, I wondered, that my future as a national media star rested on the president's participation?

Somewhere along the line, an official had told me, "Oh, he'll be there, all right, as long as there isn't a national emergency." I thought about that. I was willing to bet that the last time there had been a day without a national emergency was during some quiet week in the mid-1920s.

There were indications, of course. The Secret Service man sniffing the trees. The photographers and journalists milling around. The delay of the starting time of the race.

Expectancy hung like beads of sweat on the trees.

"And now I'd like to introduce the president . . ." an official suddenly announced during prerace introductions, ". . . of the Hagerstown Run for Fun Club." Many of us listening inhaled on the word "president."

Finally there was some commotion up the street, the sounds of people cheering. This, obviously, was the moment all of us (and especially, I thought, me) had waited for. I jogged to the starting line, thinking that President Carter would be easily visible at the front of the pack. He wasn't, so I began to scan the crowd intently, hopping up and down. Where was the man?

Finally I spotted him, near the middle of the pack, wearing a yellow headband and gray T-shirt. He looked small and vulnerable, and I felt a tinge of compassion for the man who would attempt his first organized run on this difficult course, with the whole world watching.

Perhaps this was when I felt my first tinge of guilt, too, like the tap of a friend's hand on my shoulder. I was still harboring my joke about whipping Kennedy's ass. Was it really appropriate, I wondered, to make fun of the main man this way? It began to seem slightly out of line, like making flatulent barks with one's hand at a city council meeting.

Then again, that can be funny, can't it?

When the gun fired, two thoughts went through my head: to finish in the top three, and to see Carter on the second half of this out-and-back course.

Halfway into the race, I was close to third place and looking for the president. Herb Lindsay was firmly in control of the top spot, and Dan Rincon followed. Somehow, as I continued to work on third place, I was unable to spot Carter. I wondered if there had been a problem of some sort.

At about four miles I took control of third, and finished the race in a blaze of mediocrity. I wandered back to watch Carter finish.

The next half-hour was absurdist drama. Waiting for Carter. The announcer identified the parade of finishers as best he could, while the crowd kept faithful watch for the President of the United States. A platform especially constructed for the occasion held an accordion of photographers, cameras poised and focused.

The parade of runners continued. Photographers from every major periodical and news service waited, and began to fidget slightly. Where was the guy?

A slight buzz ruffled the crew of Secret Service surrounding Rosalynn Carter. They escorted her to a limousine and left.

The announcer saw me and signaled me to come over. "He's not going to finish here," he told me quietly.

"Oh," I mumbled. "Okay, thanks."

Now what, I wondered. Am I ever going to get to meet the president, or has a few seconds at the starting line been the extent of it? I wandered off into the crowd to look for friends.

"Hey, did Phil Stewart find you yet?" came the voice of Jeff Darman as he jogged up suddenly.

"No. Why?" I asked.

"Didn't you hear what happened?" he added.

"No, what?"

"Carter had to quit. He looked horrible. Phil was running with him, and he was the only photographer there taking pictures when he dropped out."

I looked back at the platform full of photographers. They were still waiting, fidgeting even more now. I looked back at Jeff.

"You're kidding," I said as Phil came walking up, camera in hand.

I sat on the lawn listening to bluegrass music, waiting for the awards ceremony to begin. The rumors had run amok for a while, but the truth seemed to be that Jimmy Carter had overdone it a little that morning. He had dropped out, exhausted, and had gone back to Camp David. I had resigned myself to my brief glimpse of him at the start. That would have to do.

Then suddenly, like the flutter of leaves in the trees, commotion began building in the background. Reporters and photographers seemed to spout on the hillside. People turned and looked back up the hill. Jimmy Carter, the President of the United States, was walking toward the awards stand, surrounded by an entourage of newsmen, photographers, and Secret Service.

The next few minutes passed quickly. President Carter presented an award to winner Herb Lindsay, joking, "I never thought you'd beat me, Herb."

Lindsay, looking like a young senator making a nominating speech, responded by praising Carter for attempting his first race on such a difficult course.

Carter then presented the second-place award to Dan Rincon, and I began salivating. My big moment was upon me.

"And now," said the announcer, "the president will present the award to the first female finisher."

I was dumbfounded. After all this, I would not get my award from the president after all. Somehow I stayed in control. I got a good vantage point and took some pictures, struggling to convince myself that it didn't matter. Like hell it didn't.

A few minutes passed, during which Carter presented what he called "The Double-O-Seven Award" to the F.B.I. team, winner of the F.B.I.–C.I.A.–Secret Service competition. "That's not really fair, though," the president quipped, "because the Secret Service had to run with me."

I don't know exactly how to put this, but suddenly I was back in sync. In tune. On the big screen. The announcer was introducing me. The president was holding the third-place award. I began approaching the stage.

I felt slightly giddy as I stepped to the platform. President Carter awaited with my plaque. As I walked up and shook his hand, he gave me my award and asked, "What did you run in the marathon?"

I wanted to tell the whole story. About running conservatively and going for broke and getting an invitation to this race and wanting to make the awards stand and whipping Kennedy's ass. Instead I said, "2:16:40."

He told the crowd, "He just ran a marathon in two hours and sixteen minutes." He stepped back, and I stepped to the mike.

Okay, fans, there I was. My big moment. And yet somewhere between the start of this adventure and the time I got to the mike, it left me. Maybe it was never really there. Maybe I got cold feet watching the Secret Service. They seemed ready to kill without provocation, you know. But I suspect it had more to do with empathy.

The President of the United States had dropped out of his first race, exhausted, from a simple running mistake. He had gone out too hard. I knew the feeling, and I already sensed the political hay that would be harvested from his mistake. At any rate, there would be no whipping-Kennedy's-ass jokes from this kid. Not today. No.

A week later, at a sportswriters' luncheon in Spokane, I told the crowd about qualifying for the Olympic Trials at the Nike Marathon. I also told them, basically, this story, including the part about whipping Kennedy's ass.

I told them that when I got on the stage my flippancy left me, but that I did start with the line, "This is even more exciting than the first time I met Frank Shorter." I also told them that I had gone on to invite the president to the Lilac Bloomsday Run in Spokane next May, promising that the course would be flat. The second part of my speech, the invitation to a flat course, had been telecast nationally by one of the networks on the evening news.

After the luncheon, I stood outside the restaurant, talking about the marathon, the run with Carter, and my training and racing plans as I prepare for the Olympic Trials.

One of the reporters walked by, then paused. "Hey," he chimed, "you should have used that line about Kennedy. I'll bet that would have got you on all *three* networks."

(OCTOBER 1979)

Becoming Winter

THIRTY MILES north of Spokane the landscape suddenly bulges from slightly over two thousand feet to almost six thousand. Seeming vaguely misplaced among the farmlands surrounding it, Mount Spokane sits serenely, the first inkling of mountainous regions farther north and west.

In the spring and fall, fresh snow will sometimes dust the summit without sticking at lower elevations. On such days, viewed from the city, the white dome seems removed from the surrounding territory. Dazzling the eye, it strikes the imagination like the glitter of a flake of gold in a handful of sand.

From the summit of Mount Spokane the distant view of mountainous northern Idaho and the peaks of British Columbia fires the imagination. Closer in, the lakes, orchards, farms, and towns of Spokane county, and the city itself, urge introspective and retrospective thought. All in all, the scenery presents grist for the mill of serious contemplation.

Although the mountain is without snow throughout the summer, its aloof attraction remains. Knowing that it would soon be glazed with snow and therefore impassable, I set out one day this fall to run to the top, to celebrate the last remnants of warm weather.

In fact, the warm weather had finally broken, and cool rain showers visited the land below as I began my run. The rain was welcome. It ended a drought of a month-and-a-half, during which time wheat farmers had grumbled and forest rangers had nervously scanned the territory for signs of danger. Now, as nature moved into a new cycle, the foliage of Mount Spokane showed the colorful workings of autumn.

I ran with surprising ease up the hill past a picnic area where, in late August, we had celebrated after the first annual Mount Spokane Mile-High Distance Classic. Then, sitting in the sun, we had seemed to be baking atop a pyre of dry weeds and firewood. Now, as I ran past, ripe golds, browns, and a spectrum of greens leapt in the moist woods.

I continued the ascent, puffing rhythmically but feeling elated rather than winded from the climb. On the left side of the road a grouse waddled up the hill, turning when it heard me coming. Surprised, it darted left, then right, then left again, apparently forgetting that it could either fly or run to the nearby underbrush. As I ran by I looked back to see it staring dumbly after me.

Coming to the top of a steep rise, I glanced to the left, where the first good view of the land unfolded itself. Rain fell gently below, and fifty miles or so in the distance I could see Indian territory, the Colville Reservation, where I had run a seven-mile run a few months earlier.

Most of eastern Washington is extremely dry, despite the images that come to mind when people think of the state. On entering Washington from the southeast, one crosses the Columbia River and is greeted with the sight of miles and miles of sagebrush and a sign that says WELCOME TO WASHINGTON, THE EVERGREEN STATE. Nespelem, site of the Colville-Nespelem Endurance Run, is in this dry region. I had been warned ahead of time by several Indian friends to come prepared for hot weather.

The Endurance Run came on the same weekend as the Peachtree Road Race. Somehow, the invitation to run with a few dozen people on the Colville Reservation seemed more interesting than facing the staggering hordes in Atlanta.

I remembered when the invitation was first extended to me. Jim Breiler, a young Indian with black hair tied in two long braids, had come into my store in Spokane a year ago, asking to display a poster of the run.

The poster had a detailed drawing of several Indian braves running, one of them clearly in the lead.

"The drawing was done by one of our tribal artists," he told me in quiet, measured tones. "It has quite a bit of symbolism. The braves are shown running away from their families. This shows the freedom from daily routine one experiences through running."

He went on to explain the importance running used to have in the religious celebrations of the tribe, especially in connection with the fall hunting season. Then he pointed to the lead runner in the drawing. "See that?" he said. "That's Frank Shorter, dressed as an Indian." I looked. There he was all right, the gold and silver medalist, in braids, loincloth, and leggings.

"Sometime we'd like to get you to join in our run," he said quietly.

The rain that was falling as I continued running up the switchback asphalt road on Mount Spokane had been nowhere in sight when I pitched my tent the night before the Endurance Run, months earlier. But the sky had been uneasy, and there was a hint of thunderstorms brewing.

My friend Steve and I drove from the campground to Nespelem, where a large celebration was under way. Hundreds of Indians had gathered beneath an enormous canvas roof to compete in dance contests. The dance arena was surrounded by both teepees and recreational vehicles, but as each tribe chanted its songs, and the dancers circled the arena bedecked in beads and feathers, the rhythms were distinctly Indian, as ancient as the land.

When we left, the wind was gusting, the moon shone, and in the distance lightning streaked the sky.

The next morning we stood on the starting line for the run. It was warm, and in spite of the wind and lightning of the night before, no rain had fallen on Nespelem. Tim Jordan, a teammate of mine and a Colville Indian raised in Seattle, was describing the course to me.

"Just follow the main road below that ridge," he said, pointing into the distance. "When it curves around toward the main road, you'll have to take a right. On the dirt road coming back, keep zigzagging to stay on the main route. Make sure you don't head into any of the driveways to the farmhouses."

"Are there any dogs along the way?" I asked.

Tim smiled. "Yes, along the dirt road there are."

Jim Breiler walked up. He smiled at my uneasiness. "They travel in groups," he said. "We call them the Nespelem packs."

Tim watched my reaction, then said, "Don't worry. They'll chase you but they won't bite you." He paused and looked at me for a long moment, his brown eyes quietly amused. "What I should say," he added, "is that they won't bite *me*."

Reflecting on the Endurance Run as I neared the summit of Mount Spokane, I watched a tiny chipmunk skitter across the road, its tail perpendicular. I guessed that this must be its first autumn and that it was distressed by the onset of winter. Biology would prompt it to respond correctly, of course, to gather food for the winter. But it seemed now that its chipmunk mind was somehow confused as to what to do next.

My own musings were not so confused, I thought. Winter was coming, a time of frozen dormancy. Training would slow down, and my muscles would have time to regroup for the challenges that would face me next spring in my Olympic quest. Desire would have time to simmer.

It must have been the pride of native Americans to experience the kind of seasonal harmony I sensed as I reached the top of Mount Spokane. In all directions I could see the steady approach of winter.

The gold, green, and purple hues of the leaves promised that the seasonal life of the forest would return in a few months.

Meanwhile, I would continue to run along, slow mileage through the winter months, remembering the warmth of last summer on the Colville Indian Reservation, when I outran a pack of dogs and finished first. And I would nurture my Olympic dream.

After a few minutes at the summit, I headed back down the mountain. On the way I noticed a hawk drifting above me, a silhouette against the gray sky. Like a thought, like a dream, it hovered above me, effortlessly following my running.

Two days later, nine inches of snow fell on Mount Spokane in slow, lazy flakes, blanketing the mountain in winter.

(NOVEMBER 1979)

Money

IN THE SPRING OF 1976, while I was still, by profession, a sixth-grade teacher, I enjoyed a three-day weekend in Eugene that resulted in a spot on the U.S. Olympic team. News of my third-place finish in the Olympic Trials Marathon preceded my return to Spokane, and on Monday morning Loma Vista Elementary School was ablaze with excitement.

The enthusiasm of the kids snowballed with the enthusiasm of the teachers throughout the week, and on Friday the principal decided to direct all that energy into the first pep rally in the school's history.

The kids, never having attended a pep rally before, filed into the gym as they had always been instructed to, quietly, with a minimum of disturbance. I stood in the hall at the rear of the gym, listening to the muffled sounds, wondering what kind of somber rally this was going to be.

After a few minutes, the principal stepped to the front, grinning.

He realized that, after years of trying to calm this assembled mob, he was now living the disciplinarian's dream. It was his duty to incite a riot. He grinned devilishly as he shouted to the throng, "Come on, what's the matter? This is a pep rally. Let's get excited!"

Startled, the kids didn't respond at first. Then slowly, from somewhere, a chant began.

"We want Kardong. We want Kardong. We want Kardong." It grew louder.

I have never been in the situation, but I know what a lynch mob sounds like. It sounds like this: "We want Kardong. We want Kardong! We want Kardong!"

In their first rally, the kids welcomed me onto the Olympic team with the kind of chant they had heard on the evening news and the Saturday monster movie.

"We want Kardong!"

I shivered and walked into the gym.

The eerie chant that greeted me that day will be etched in my mind forever, symbolizing as it does the high-spirited but threatening expectations of sports enthusiasts of any age. I would discover over and over again in the ensuing months that an Olympian is both encouraged and expected to live up to Olympic billing.

A second aspect of that pep rally has also stayed with me. After I walked into the gym and said a few words of thanks, the student-body president came up and handed me a gift. It was an old sock filled with coins, tied in a knot at the top. The money had been collected from the students to help send me to Montreal.

The gesture was genuine, and I appreciated it. But beyond that, the scene symbolized a set of beliefs and values about money and the Olympic Games, all of which continually force their way into my mind during these months preceding the Olympic Trials.

Somewhere in memory are scenes from a movie I once saw about a young Cuban marathoner who was sent by his town, at great sacrifice, to the St. Louis Olympic Games. Along the way he was cheated out of his money, and he ended up in Miami, broke and ashamed. To reconcile his loss, he ran the rest of the way to St.

Louis, in street shoes, and got there just in time to enter the marathon, determined to win.

The Cuban was on his way to a clear victory in the race until an announcer mistakenly broadcast the news that someone else had won. Crestfallen, he dropped out, and though he discovered the error soon afterward, it was too late. He made a heroic attempt to regain his position, but finished out of the money.

So to speak.

I probably wouldn't like the movie if I saw it now. The guy probably ran like an offensive tackle and wore black socks. But at the time it was as symbolic a picture as there could be. Money and society. Sacrifice and suffering. One man's determination to be heroic in spite of the pitfalls of evil money.

I used to take great pride in the monastic exercise of long-distance running, back before Charlie's Angels and the president took a shine to the activity. If I was hassled by people as I ran, the experience simply reminded me of the depths of my heroism. If I was short on funds because I wanted to pursue an athletic fantasy, it simply strengthened my desire to succeed.

My teammates and I overstated our disdain for monetary rewards in those days, and we emphasized our ability to tolerate the meager but pure lifestyle that would allow us time to develop as runners.

On track trips we would receive five dollars each for dinner, then pool it to buy a loaf of bread and some sliced meat. We'd each make about four dollars on the deal and gloat over our gain.

At buffets we considered ourselves terrors. We knew the owner of any all-you-can-eat place would increase his buffet price in the week following our rampaging, gluttonous visit. We got triple our money's worth, or so we thought.

Once, at the AAU cross-country championships in Philadelphia, my friend Brook and I arrived at the postrace buffet after most of the food had been eaten. All that was left was a little bread and some half-melted ice cream. Undaunted, Brook began spreading ice cream on bread, and we were soon able to enjoy homemade ice-cream sandwiches.

As mooching goes, Brook was one of the best. He has eaten more free meals at more dormitories around the country than anyone, ever. Once, to get a free lunch, he walked through a dormitory kitchen, past unquestioning cooks, servers, and assorted staff, innocently avoiding the meal-card puncher, who would have thrown him out. Another time he walked out of a cafeteria with an enormous serving bowl filled with raisins. One summer, to avoid paying rent, he stayed in the bushes behind a dormitory at Stanford, rolling his sleeping bag up every morning when the gardener woke him. His clothes were hung neatly on hangers in the branches around him.

"I don't do those things anymore," he admitted to me recently. "I saved some money, of course, but I really did things like that so I could tell stories about it later."

Perhaps we weren't that hard up. We had some money and we lived reasonably well. Still, we weren't actually making money by running. We did sacrifice to continue, and there was a certain purity in that fact that we relished.

Things have changed dramatically since then. In the last few years, with the increase in running interest, the amount of money available to people associated with running has also increased. Whether it's the shoe business, the clinic business, or the race business, the money is there. It's possible to live comfortably as nothing more or less than a runner.

A college teammate of mine who had been out of the running scene for a few years was intrigued to listen to conversations at a prerace party recently.

"The predominant topic didn't surprise me," he said. "It was racing. But do you know what was second? Business. Everyone was talking about their stores or running gear."

This is no surprise to those who have been close to the sport recently, but it would amaze the majority of people in the country, people who still consider amateur sports to be full of amateurs.

I was talking with a man the other day about some of the money available, in a variety of forms, to amateur runners. When the extent of it sank in, he suddenly exclaimed, "But that totally destroys the Olympic ideal!"

"Not the Olympic ideal," I responded, "only the amateur ideal!"

And as I train in these months before the Olympic Trials, the fact that I'm heavily into the running business does not really diminish the fact that I'm essentially, still, into running itself.

I've spent fifteen years of my life trying to perfect a talent I have for moving quickly over the earth's surface. I'm still attuned to that activity itself, even though I'm earning a living because of it. There is a distinction between running for money and running for running's own sake, of course, but the money has nothing to do with it. You feel the distinction at gut level.

We don't lose respect for a professional athlete because he gets money for his sport. We lose respect for him if, and only if, he ceases to love his profession.

In my pre-Olympic training, I have to keep sorting this out in my mind. I run thinking of runners who have failed because they are distracted by money, and I try to steer a course that remains committed to an Olympic ideal of athletic excellence, regardless of the money or lack of it. In this society, that isn't easy.

About a month ago, a man came into my store and spoke with my partner about a sports extravaganza he was organizing. He wanted our store to be one of a hundred participating businesses, each of which would pay three hundred fifty dollars for a display in a large arena. Three professional athletes would be brought to town to shake hands and sign autographs for what he hoped would be twenty thousand participants. From a total budget of around one hundred thousand dollars, five thousand would go to the Olympic fund-raising organization.

When I heard about this I began seething. For days I ran distracted by the man's scheme. Distracted by money.

He called back a week later. "Your partner says you have some reservations about the event," he said.

I was calm, I think. "Yes, I do. I think that five thousand dollars to the Olympic fund represents a pretty low proportion of your total budget."

"Well," he replied, "I know it may seem like it, but you have to realize that our expenses are enormous. We had to pay Jim Zorn an extra three thousand dollars just to stick around for three extra hours."

This was the wrong thing to tell me. It reminded me that while amateur purists, which I no longer am, are sitting around discussing how to prevent money from going to amateurs, the real rip-off of the sport is occurring at another level.

"Look at it from my perspective," I told the man. "You're paying three professional athletes, only one of whom is in an Olympic sport, five thousand dollars a day plus expenses. You're paying a mere five thousand dollars out of your total budget to the Olympic fund. And not only are you asking me to show up for free, you'd actually like my store to pay three hundred fifty dollars for the privilege."

"All right," he said, after a pause, "we'd be glad to give you the booth space for nothing."

There it was. A magnanimous concession from a representative of the business world to me, a representative of the Olympic world. I thought of the years of training I had put in and the months of hard training ahead. I thought of the thousands of runners who are still unable to afford the cost of pursuing their love, running, even while the money proliferates. I thought of that day four years ago when the mob yelled "We want Kardong!" and handed me a sock filled with money. I thought of the crust of bread, free booth space at a sports extravaganza, that had just fallen in front of me. I considered my own lost innocence.

"I'll tell you what," I replied. "I'll be glad to show up for whatever Zorn is getting."

The laughter on the other end of the line was deafening.

He thought I was kidding.

The Runner Crumbles

AFTER more than a week of feverish, blurred, coughing, snot-blowing incapacitation, I was finally back on my feet. Barely. It had been one nasty week of illness.

One week earlier I was telling myself that, through some mysterious process, the infection that was beginning to throttle my throat would soon be gone. I can run a hundred miles a week with relative ease, so there was no reason to think that a simple virus would frustrate my body's ability to battle it.

I was mistaken.

During the first day of this disease, I thought that a good night's sleep would bring me around. No. When I called in sick the second day, I made plans to run the following day. No way. The third day, weak and coughing, I bailed out of my training plans and went to bed early, determined to get a few miles in the fourth day. The fourth day I bundled up and ran a half mile before I turned around and ran home, wheezing and coughing and cursing.

By this time it was my cough-racked chest that bore the brunt of the infection's attack on my body. I felt that a viral Rocky Balboa had been punching me in the lower middle part of my rib cage for fifteen rounds. Somewhere during the bout he must have scored a few hits on my face too, as evidenced by the nosebleed I suffered one night.

And then finally, after multiple attempts, I was back on my feet, feeling well enough to try running. I had been down for a count of eight. Eight long, miserable days.

The books all say that someone who runs as diligently as I do is addicted to running. If denied my daily fix, I would reveal the usual symptoms of narcotics withdrawal.

It is a tribute to the mean punch of that tiny, viral Rocky that

I never once exhibited any such signs of addiction. Cold turkey from running was easy. Mentally I felt I should try to run, but physically I had no desire. None.

When I finally recovered, though, and got dressed for a ten-mile run, it did seem good to be back at it. To have beaten the flu bug. To be breathing more like my old self again, as they say.

And then I began running.

You wouldn't think that in a week I could have forgotten how to run—which foot goes first, and which leg to use after the left. Which muscles to call into action in which order. Was it hamstring-quads-calf or quads-hamstring-calf? I had forgotten.

On top of that, there was very little muscle tone to rely on. I felt flabby, uncoordinated, tired, and out-of-place. If someone had seen me, I thought, they would have noticed the difference. One week of flu had made me a novice runner. Was this my condition only five months before the Olympic Trials?

The condition I was in, and the proximity to the 1980 Olympic Trials, brought back chilling memories of 1972 and my first attempt at making the Olympic team.

In the year prior to that, I was in my final chapter of college life. I had run some successful races, finishing near the top of the national ladder several times, but also running more than my share of mediocre races. Graduation from college brought the usual flux of confusion as to future plans.

Should I continue running competitively, even though I had no reason to consider myself anything more than a better-than-average runner? Should I try for a spot on the Olympic team, a spot I had no good reason to believe I could reach? Or should I start doing whatever it was I was going to do for a living? Teaching? Graduate school? Or what?

Somewhere, while I was trying to decide, I read an interview with Frank Shorter, who was then on the upward spiral of a running career that would bring him the Olympic gold medal. He described being at a similar crossroads in his life a few years earlier, and told how he had decided to put all his energy into his training. "I didn't want to quit," he was quoted as saying, "and have to tell myself for the rest of my life, 'Well, maybe I could have been . . .' "

The quote hit home. I made up my mind to take the next year off from everything but running. To organize my life around a systematic, insufferably dedicated training program and see what would happen. If an undistracted immersion in running didn't bring results, nothing would.

So I began my golden year. I was living in California, where I had plenty of good weather and training opportunities. I didn't work. I ate, ran, and rested.

In the morning I'd get up about eleven and head out for ten miles. Upon returning, I'd eat a big breakfast, then I'd shower and eat a big lunch.

In the afternoon I'd sit down in an enormous bean-bag chair and read for an hour or two, then I'd put in another ten-mile run or a hard track workout and wander home to watch reruns of *Dragnet* on television before dinner.

After dinner I'd read a little more, peruse a few Zap Comix and discuss their significance with my roommates ("What does it all mean, Mr. Natural?"), then settle down for *The Tonight Show*. At 1:00 A.M. it was time for bed.

The next morning at eleven the cycle began again. And with slight modifications and embellishments it went on day after day after glorious, self-indulgent day.

My mileage increased from the ninety miles per week of my college days to over a hundred and forty. It was hard-core training, but I seemed to be tolerating it and getting stronger.

The long-range goal was, of course, the Olympic Trials, but in the meantime I took what came along, including indoor running and my first marathon. One weekend they occurred within twelve hours of each other, as I ran my fastest indoor two-mile Saturday night and my first marathon the next morning. I was showing great promise but little sense.

That was also the winter I qualified for my first U.S. team, to compete indoors against the U.S.S.R. in the three-mile. I ended up rooming with miler Bruce Fischer from Syracuse, who was also on his first U.S. team. After getting our team uniforms, we strutted around in front of the mirror in U.S. colors, acting like ten-year-olds wearing adult clothes, giggling self-consciously.

Everything was on schedule for an Olympic berth. It was early in the year, I had not yet begun speed training, and yet I was running better than ever. I had made a U.S. team and had had my first intoxicating taste of international competition. After the U.S.–U.S.S.R. indoor, I got back to a schedule of high mileage and moderate track work and began looking toward the Olympic Trials.

A month later, competing in my first outdoor race, I ran tired. The sluggishness was due, I was sure, to the heavy training I was doing. When I lightened up and began to peak, the quickness would return.

It didn't. On successive weekends I raced slower and slower. After one especially bad mile race in Modesto, I decided that something might physically be wrong. I went to see the doctor.

"You have mono," he pronounced, after testing.

I sat stunned.

Eight years later the effect of those three words—you have mono—is almost as strong as it was in 1972. As I sat in the doctor's office, I tried to relate to the news as I felt one should always relate to life's great practical jokes. I became detached, analytical, philosophical.

"Life is unfair. But that's not cause for despair," I mumbled in my mind. "Whoever's testing you is watching now. Relax. That's the way it goes." I searched for the right line. "Imagine you're a character in a book. Enjoy the irony." I groped for truth in sayings I remembered from the locker-room wall. "Champions are gracious and humble. Lock your lockers!"

Something worked. One of those lines I spoke to myself, or a combination of them, or the fact that I really did appreciate the irony of having spent a year training for nothing, kept me cool. I decided to ride out the illness and enter the Olympic Trials anyway.

I remember now how I felt, after two weeks of infected incarceration in my house, when I first took to the streets again. I felt just how I felt after my recent eight-day battle with the flu. For two weeks I ran five miles a day, relearning how to run, searching for lost muscle tone, begging for a return of fitness.

The results in the Olympic Trials were predictable. I ran two mediocre races, finishing well out of third place, well off the Olympic team. It was an exercise in humility and how quickly one can fall from fitness to fatness.

When I hear any of the great runners, jumpers, or throwers of this country, someone people believe has a great chance for an Olympic gold medal, make the comment that their first concern is making the U.S. team, I now realize that they're not spouting false modesty. Rather, they're revealing a realistic appreciation of the fickle cards dealt by Lady Luck.

This time, in 1980, I'll recover from my illness in time to return to top form. But as I train with Olympic hopes, the specter of a drastic reversal in my conditioning and a fall from competitive fitness runs beside me. A carefully constructed training program is balanced precariously when one considers the chances of running amok with luck.

A rock lies in wait to turn an ankle. A car driver forgets to look to the right as a runner approaches. A muscle in action begins to pull. Billions of viral Rockys look for a body to punch.

It's all part of the Olympic game. Years of training. Hours of dreaming. And knowing it can all come down to an unfortunate, untimely, unbelievable stroke of bad luck.

(FEBRUARY 1980)

Speedy Goes to the Olympics—Alone

I WAS REASSURED, as I sat watching the Winter Olympics on TV, to be continually reminded that Sammy Davis, Jr., and his good friend Speedy Alka-Seltzer would be attending the Olympic Games. I smiled as I watched them board the plane, bound for Moscow, and heard Speedy's uplifting voice. I was reassured to know that our country really would be represented at the 1980 Olympic Games.

"They're going to Lake Placid, not Moscow," I was told flatly, unsympathetically, when I revealed the good news to a friend of mine.

"Oh, no," I countered. "If it was the Winter Olympics they'd say so. You heard them: 'Alka-Seltzer is going to the 1980 Olympic Games.' "

Thus I held on to hope, while the Soviet government continued to ignore President Carter's deadline for exiting Afghanistan.

At this point I have a confession to make. My life does not revolve around the Olympic Games. In looking over some of the articles I've written in this Olympic series for *Running Times*, I realize that I've sometimes given that impression.

That impression is poetic license, a prerequisite for the kind of article I've been asked to do. A way of increasing the interest of the reader in the ongoing challenge to make the Olympic team. A method of focusing my own thoughts on what I'm writing.

That impression is false. I can live without a hug from Misha the bear. I really can.

In the past few weeks I've been approached by friends and well-wishers who want to know what I think about the boycott. Whatever answer I give, they invariably put on a face of grave mourning and then ask, "What are you going to do now?"

Well, dear friends, here's what I'm going to do now: Get up in the morning, run, eat, listen to the radio, go to work, eat lunch, run, watch TV, and go to bed. Go to movies, plays, concerts, games, exhibitions, discos, and races. Ski, swim, run, golf, hike, read, and sleep. Work and play. Run and rest. Sit in a nice steamy hot tub with my friends. And so on.

A lot goes on in life.

I was in Florida a few weeks ago for the Gasparilla Distance Classic, and as I sat at dinner the evening before the race, in walked Ed Ayres, *Running Times*'s editor-in-chief. Perry White to me. Ed is the one who first suggested this Olympic series to me. He's the one who decided the Olympics was a sufficient excuse to allow a former Olympic marathoner like myself to write convoluted, self-indulgent pieces like this one. Ed gets the same phone call every month ("Ed, it's going to be a little late again."). He always responds with infinite patience.

"What do I do now?" I asked him in feigned exasperation.

"What do you mean?" he responded.

"You hired me to do an Olympic series, and now there aren't going to be any Olympics. I'm out of a job!"

He leaned back in his chair, exuding wisdom. "Well, I disagree," he began. "As I see it, there are several interesting approaches to the situation. . . ." And on he went.

After a minute or two I broke in, "But, Ed, I had this great article all ready. You see I got on this flight to Denver and Dylan got on the plane. Bob Dylan! I had the whole article planned."

Ed smiled. He knows me pretty well by now, and he knew the boycott wouldn't end the Olympic series I was writing.

And now, by convincing you that life goes on without the Olympics, I'm giving the impression that I'm not especially interested in them, and that the boycott is a minor issue in my estimation. That's not true either.

I've had this dream, this infatuation, this inebriation with the Olympics for many years. For at least the last ten years I've been an Olympic hopeful and have worked for a lifestyle that would make Olympic participation a possibility.

After one successful try in 1976, I was convinced I had an opportunity to win a medal in 1980. Much of what I've been doing has been predicated on that. All of my training for the last year has been woven around the Olympics, focused on that goal.

I had a chance. A chance, however slim, is worth nurturing.

In my article last month I spoke of a bout I had just had with the flu, an illness that seemed to set my training back twenty years. I described my Olympic bid in 1972, when I was running better than ever until mononucleosis knocked me down a few weeks before the trials. I was philosophical about the role that illness and injury play in the Olympics and about years of work that dissolve in the presence of bad luck.

And as I sat watching the Winter Olympics between Alka-Seltzer commercial breaks, I heard Dick Button bemoan the fact, for the umpteenth time, that Tai Babalonia and Randy Gardner were out of the pairs figure skating because of Randy's pulled groin muscle.

"Sure they moan about that," said a friend of mine. "But who's moaning about the way the government pulled the groin of every potential competitor in the summer Olympics?"

I love that phrase. Pulled their groins . . .

In fact, a lot of people were bemoaning the boycott. I had spent several days writing a statement for *Footnotes* magazine against the boycott, but in doing so I felt helpless. Like a vegetarian addressing the Cattlemen's Association. Like a Quaker addressing the Joint Chiefs of Staff. Like the President of the United States addressing a group of militant Iranian students. My argument seemed wasted— or worse, maybe I was wrong.

The argument goes around and around.

Politics and sport don't mix. Politics and sport have always mixed. The boycott would be ineffective. The boycott would hit the Russians where it hurts, in their national pride. Afghanistan is no different from Vietnam. An Olympic boycott would have no impact on Soviet actions in Afghanistan. A boycott would show the world where we stand. Sport should not be a weapon of national political systems. It always has been. And on and on.

One thing left me especially bitter, though, and seemed to cut through the arguments of both sides.

For as long as I can remember, for as long as I've been paying attention, the U.S. Government has denied any responsibility for amateur sport. No financial subsidies in the country, said Congress, because sport is not government business. Even people who felt slighted by this governmental indifference seemed able to justify it by arguing that at least it left our athletic system free of political interference.

When President Carter put a grain embargo in effect, he agreed to pay farmers over two billion dollars for the grain originally bound for the U.S.S.R. When President Carter declared the Olympic boycott, he offered nothing to either Olympic athletes or national sports-governing bodies by way of compensation, except for a pitiful "alternate Olympics."

While grain farmers can go back to work, accepting subsidies even while the price of a bushel of their produce has risen from $4.02 to $4.25, amateur athletes can ready themselves for the time when once again they will be ignored by their government. They can train in obscurity, make financial sacrifices, and hope that their government doesn't need them for another political statement in 1984.

In dealing with all this, I find myself retreating to sarcasm. I was asked recently what I thought about an alternate Olympics.

"Well," I replied, "I'd only favor such a thing on two conditions. First, the U.S. should not participate if England is involved, unless they get their troops out of Northern Ireland. Second, the participants in such a competition should all be politicians. Carter against Brezhnev, Thatcher against Gandhi, et cetera."

But then life does go on. All those Misha souvenirs will find a home somewhere, if only in the L.A. dump. Maybe they'll become like Edsels, or pet rocks. Wonderful absurdity.

In the meantime, while all this has been going on, a cycle has been completed here in Spokane. Crocuses and tulips have begun to push up through thawed patches of earth. I heard birds singing the other morning when I got up to run. As I laced up my running shoes, I wondered whether I needed gloves anymore. The nasty spell of winter had been broken.

As I headed down the road to a run along the river, the problems of the Olympics seemed to melt away, and a musical jingle pranced its way through my mind.

"Plop, plop, fizz, fizz. Oh, what a relief it is. Plop, plop, fizz, fizz . . ."

Thank God for spring and the relief of long, slow distance.

(MARCH 1980)

Spring 1980

THERE IS no subtlety to spring.

It leaps from nowhere, surprising us even though we've learned to expect it at the same time every year. Suddenly, we wake up and realize that a robin is singing outside the window. We can't remember when the robins left, and we're not exactly sure where they've been. All we know is that they're back. Spring has arrived.

The surprises are continual. As I headed out for a twenty-mile run last Sunday, I noticed that the crocuses next door were almost ready to bloom. They looked as if they'd been up for a long time, and yet this was the first time I'd seen them. This was embarrassing, since I'd been watching for them daily.

The line, "Black earth becoming yellow crocus is unmitigated hocus-pocus," words of poet Piet Hein, floated to mind as I ran down toward the river.

The day before had featured the kind of weather people around here insist on calling unusual, even though there is no weather more typical at this time of year. During my morning run, the gray skies turned to rain, then to brilliant sunshine, aided by a strong wind out of the southwest. At night the wind was still blowing, but a nearly full moon promised unprecipitative conditions for my evening run. Nevertheless, it began snowing after thirty minutes and had piled nearly an inch on the ground by the time I returned. Fortunately, I had at least avoided scheduling a run for that afternoon, when the hailstorm hit.

The Sunday I noticed the crocuses, though, was a day of bright skies and gentle breezes, just a few degrees away from being truly warm. It was the type of day that lives in optimistic memories as "typical" of spring.

The snow that had fallen the night before had melted, leaving no trace, and the change in the weather was so complete that it was hard to believe the previous day's conditions had existed at all. It was as if Saturday's bizarre combination of wind, snow, rain, hail, and sun were the final throes of Mother Nature's exorcism. The devil of winter had finally departed, leaving spring warm and peaceful.

As I ran next to the river, the smell of pine trees warmed by the sun was another surprise to the senses. I made a mental note to record this as the olfactory equivalent of robins and crocuses. It was the first spring smell I had noticed.

It's nearly impossible to feel emotionally down on that kind of day. As I ran along, I felt lighter and more relaxed than I had in days. A week-long sluggishness seemed to lift, and I began to think I would complete the twenty miles without any fatigue at all.

In the last few weeks I had been feeling better and better about my conditioning, and as I ran along I was reassured to think back on the previous week's total mileage and intensity. It had been exactly the kind of pre-Olympic Trials training I wanted to pursue. If anything was going to put me on the Olympic team again, the kind of program I was on was the key. All the elements of successful training had been falling neatly into place.

But as I ran along, the inevitable good feelings of spring were interrupted by the realization that, at least in terms of the Olympics, this training was wasted. U.S. athletes would not be competing in Moscow.

I can live without the Olympics. I'm not happy about the boycott, but I'll survive.

On the other hand, perhaps influenced by the inevitable optimism of the season, people keep telling me these days that the U.S. will have its team in Moscow after all. Somehow, absurdly, this keeps me hoping.

"I can feel it in my guts," a friend told me a while ago. "We're going to the Olympics."

"How do you figure?" I asked. "Carter can't change his mind now. He's backed into a corner."

"I know that," he responded. "But I still think we'll go. Something will happen."

"Is there any reason to believe that?" I asked in amazement.

"I can feel it in my guts," he replied.

Maybe he's right, I thought, as I ran along. Maybe there'll be a dramatic change in Soviet intentions and actions in Afghanistan. Maybe the wild daisies won't grow this year.

I looked over to woods on the left, where in a few weeks the yellow daisies would ignite the forest floor with splashes of color. They'd be there all right.

It's hard these days to know just how to relate to the Olympics. Are they a dead issue, or should I hold on to the notion that something may happen?

I read the other day that Bill Rodgers finally gave up on his Olympic dream and was putting all his eggs in the Boston Marathon basket. Certainly a reasonable thing to do, considering the position he's in. Boston means much more to him for many reasons, and with the politicians tinkering with the Olympics, who could question his decision?

But I was on the phone with a friend recently, and the subject of Frank Shorter came up.

"Frank's running at Buffalo," he told me.

"What?" I said. "What for? He doesn't know something we don't, does he?"

"I don't think so," he said. "But you know how lucky Frank is. He'll probably be the only athlete to show up in Buffalo just as the Russians leave Afghanistan."

And so it goes. As I ran along, well into that twenty-miler on the first day of spring, the climate and season seemed out of place with the unhopeful signs on the Olympic horizon.

The warmth, the first flowers, the green buds, the pleasant smells all pointed to a renewal of things unseen for months. The increased daylight hours meant a departure from night running. Unsubtle spring was crying for rebirth and enlightenment, while the Olympic spirit seemed to be heading for a winter engulfed in darkness.

Running that day, I realized how out of tune the season was with the Olympic situation. I wanted to believe that the painful wrenchings of the past few months in the Olympic arena were like the weather conditions of the previous day. Like Saturday's wind, rain, hail, and snow, perhaps the Olympics' recent throes were actually the birth pangs of a better day. But deep down I doubted even that.

Somewhere in my head a memory jostled loose and rose to mind. It was in Montreal in 1976, in the main stadium. The Olympic flame, symbol of the Olympic spirit, had been ignited in Greece, beamed by satellite to Ottawa, rekindled, and delivered by relay runners to Montreal. There it burned, watching over the Games.

During a violent rainstorm, what to many Olympic aficionados must have seemed a religious catastrophe occurred as the flame sputtered out.

When the storm was over, while people speculated on what should be done to preserve the sanctity of the Olympic symbol, an official was hoisted to the level of the cauldron, where he flicked his BiC and got the flame going again.

Was it that easy to rekindle the sacred flame? I wonder these days, with all the talk of an alternate Olympics, whether the official with his lighter in Montreal wasn't a good symbol for the emotional sensitivity of those who seek to set up the alternate Games.

The image of the flame in Montreal stuck with me as I ran along the river. The story of the drowned Olympic fire did not end with the BiC flick.

Somewhere beneath the stadium, in a room safe from the rain, another flame, also ignited by the original from Greece, was kept burning, just in case. Someone had obviously been thinking ahead. The BiC flame was extinguished and the torch relighted with the real flame. The Games went on.

Concern for the "sanctity" of the Olympic torch may certainly be considered compulsive, unnecessary, or just plain silly. But the symbolic importance of people protecting the flame should not be overlooked, especially during spring days of compelling optimism.

I ended my twenty-miler exhausted, but inspired by the notion of rebirth and the return of light. My hope these days is that the Olympic spirit, an ideal that is seldom achieved but that should be constantly pursued, is protected from the prevailing climate of Olympic

cynicism. Whatever the outcome of the current storm over the political implications of international athletic competition, we may hope
that when it's over, someone from somewhere will relight the flame,
with the fervor of a religious zealot who will not let a holy thing
die.

(APRIL 1980)

Off the Track

I HAD NOT ESPECIALLY RELISHED this trip I was on, and now, frustrated by a cancelled flight in trying to reach Colorado Springs, I
stared, fuming, out the picture windows at the jets landing at Sta-
pleton Airport in Denver. Outside, nature itself was fuming, trying
to ignite a storm in the sky.

It was to be a weekend of difficult decisions and indecipherable
omens. As I stood watching the late-afternoon sky, I tried to decide
whether to go on a run from the airport, with all the confusion that
entailed, or take my chances as a wait-listed passenger on the next
flight to Colorado Springs.

If I made the next flight, I would arrive almost as originally
scheduled and run when I got there. If I didn't get on, though, I
would have to wait, and possibly wait again, and maybe again, and
in the waiting process my afternoon run would have dissolved.

I decided to take my chances at waiting anyway, and wandered
to the ice-cream shop to kill a few minutes and cool my temper
before heading to the gate.

No matter how often I fly, I never seem to remember air travel's
ability to be inconsistent and enigmatic. The flight from Spokane
to Colorado Springs is a short two-step affair, and I was convinced
I could fly there, make my opinion known to the U.S. Olympic
Committee delegates who were gathering to vote on the boycott,
and fly home without missing a beat. Or a workout.

Thus, when Rocky Mountain Airlines cancelled the flight from

Denver to Colorado Springs, it was more than an inconvenience. It was a break in my schedule, a threat to my training, and a further insult to my aspirations. No matter that there was no one to blame nor any explanation for the cancelled flight. Somewhere, I felt, someone was manipulating things.

I headed to the gate and handed the man my ticket. He added my name to a wait-list that was longer than the runway. Discouraged, I nevertheless decided to give patience a chance. I waited.

Fifteen minutes before flight time, the announcement was made that, due to a late-arriving plane, the flight I was waiting to board would also be late. Now I was waiting for a plane that might be really late. My opportunity to get a run in was disappearing. Frustrated and fuming again, I headed back to the other concourse.

If nothing else, I decided, I would run ten miles that day.

There is something unnerving about trying to change clothes in an airport rest room. The stall is never quite big enough. There's no seat cover to sit on, only the horseshoe lid. There's no clean place to step barefooted as you're changing shoes and socks. And all that inconvenience costs a dime.

Worst of all, though, being a paranoid at heart, I kept imagining that someone with a police badge would burst in on me in the middle of things and scream, "All right, pervert, what's going on in here?"

As I sat awkwardly trying to get my shoes and socks on, I imagined the words I would say to the man who would certainly show up soon to make the arrest. "I'm an Olympic contender!" I would scream back. "How dare you burst in when my pants are down!"

Avoiding that embarrassment, I left the men's room, checked my clothes into a locker, and stared out at the wind-choked clouds. It hadn't rained yet, but an hour of running would give time for anything to happen. If I got caught in a rainstorm, the ensuing chills I developed would not have the luxury of a hot shower. I decided to chance it anyway.

Out the door and running, I began to feel better. I headed away from the airport toward open space, found some railroad tracks with a dirt access road, and was soon striding along in relative comfort.

Though I felt my decision to run then rather than wait for another flight had been correct, I had misgivings. The information was unclear and the evidence conflicting. The decision had, in the final analysis, been more emotion than reason.

I tried to find some rational support for my choice, but I had little luck there. I seemed more at ease with reading the omens. It was a good omen, certainly, that thunderstorms in the surrounding areas were avoiding the region where I ran. God was protecting me. A bad omen, though, that the wind was blowing strongly in my face. Like Captain Ahab, I was fighting a head wind. Was this a metaphor for my goal that weekend of turning the USOC against the boycott? Was I pursuing an evil purpose, an unnatural force of destruction?

Suddenly a jackrabbit darted across the tracks ahead of me. Four rabbit's feet. That was obviously good. A half mile later, though, a magpie flew along next to me, white tail feather flashing. Nasty, flesh-eating bird. A bad omen.

Entering a railroad tunnel further on, I was weighing the pros and cons of the boycott issue, trying to decide how to deal with the ambiguities and present a clear picture to the USOC delegates. As I ran, just when things were darkest, another omen surfaced in the form of light . . . at the end of the tunnel. There was no particular light in my mind, however, as the Olympic question remained hazy. I looked toward the light at the end of the tunnel again and noticed a railroad signal—red. Bad omen.

A red light at the end of the tunnel. Who could sort that one out?

And so it went throughout the run, with one symbol conflicting with the next. Perhaps the only clear sign all day was that I was able to return safely to the airport only minutes before the wind-brewing sky began blizzarding in white anger.

I decided to face the rest of the trip dressed in the red training suit I had run in. Removing my good clothes from the locker, I headed to the check-in desk. I had been guaranteed a seat on the 8:00 P.M. flight.

I called ahead to friends in Colorado Springs and left a message that I'd be in on the next plane. Twenty minutes later the flight was cancelled.

As I stood waiting for further information at the airline desk, two men dressed in military garb made the announcement that they were renting a car. Anyone who wanted to cash in their tickets and drive to Colorado Springs could join them. The girl at the airline desk let it be known that she would try to get us on another flight if we wanted. Another decision to be made on insufficient data, but I was getting used to it.

I was soon on my way, by car, to my destination.

My traveling companions were all military men, past or present. In the back seat on the driver's side was a private in the Air Force. He was returning from a month-long vacation in his home state of Florida, and when he talked, he did so in the slowest drawl possible, with frequent stutters.

Next to him was a commander in the Air Force, a black man who spoke intently of unimaginable atrocious foods. As the guest of various families around the world, he had eaten virtually everything that moved: snakes, birds, dogs, large insects, and of course everyone's favorite, monkeys. His descriptions were detailed enough to encourage me to stare out the window at the swirling snow, trying not to listen.

On his right was a salesman of some sort, who shared joyously in the others' tales of life in Korea, which the private described as "A land of s-s-s-sliding doors, h-h-h-heated f-f-f-floors, and s-s-s-s-s-slanted whores." Everyone seemed to think that was hilarious.

I sat in the front and joined very little in the conversation. Surprisingly, during an hour-and-a-half of driving, no one asked me who I was, where I was from, or why I was going to Colorado Springs. A man in a red suit owes some sort of explanation, wouldn't you think?

The final member of our group was the driver, a commander in the Naval Reserve. I was surprised that the Navy needed forces in the middle of Colorado, but I didn't ask for an explanation. I still wonder.

He was, though, the perfect man for the driver's seat. No Captain

Ahab, he was as cool as the weather, piloting our Chevy through the snow and ice, unruffled when our windshield wipers stopped working, and quiet as the hum of the heater while our visibility shrank, and shrank, and shrank.

I sat staring ahead, looking for whatever mines might lie in our path.

"Whe-whe-when I g-g-g-get in t-t-tonight . . ." the private began.

"I love the way he talks," the monkey-eating commander giggled.

"I-I-I-I am g-g-g-g-going to t-t-t-tell my s-s-s-s-s-s-sergeant that I-I-I-I rode to C-C-Colorado S-S-Springs with t-t-t-two c-c-c-c-commanders, and he-he-he'll j-just sh-sh-sh . . ."

"Look out on your left!" I shouted to our driver.

A camper had overturned on the road ahead, in our lane. Responding calmly to the danger, the naval commander turned to avoid it. The car began fishtailing on what turned out to be a sheet of ice.

We swerved once to the right and once to the left. At that point, I thought we were going to come out of the slide, but instead we kept turning all the way around, and I saw myself staring at two lanes of approaching traffic, as the commander spoke what might have been the last words spoken by anyone on that vessel.

"Hang on men," he said, cool to the end. "I think we're going down."

In my last thoughts before we turned into the ditch, thoughts that might have been my last, two themes emerged, instantaneous and complete.

One was the realization that the situation I was in was serious. I had slipped icily off the road before, years ago, but then it had been fun. This time, the thought that struck me was that I would soon, very likely, be in big trouble. Maybe dead. I experienced a calm, peaceful fear.

The other thought was that after all this trouble, indecision, misdirection, and confusion in trying to communicate my thoughts and feelings to the USOC delegates, I was instead going to die in a car with a bunch of imbeciles who probably thought the boycott was the best idea since roast monkey.

And thus our car headed for the brink.

I did not die. I believe we came close. But as it turned out, we didn't even get hurt. We were able to push the car back onto the road and continue on our way.

When I got to Colorado Springs I was exhausted. I told of my adventures to a few friends, was briefed on the latest developments in the boycott, and went to bed.

The next morning I watched delegates from roller skating, baseball, tennis, the YMCA, the CYO, and others in the process of deciding the future of my sport. The decision must have been difficult—I've grappled with the complexities of the boycott myself— and yet somehow the final vote seemed to come easily.

I had had trouble deciphering the meaning behind the ominous forces that stormed in Denver the day before, but there was no confusion as to the force controlling the vote in Colorado Springs. For better or worse, the force was presidential, and only a few delegates chose to sail against the wind.

In the week preceding the vote, delegates had been individually called by representatives of the White House, Olympic donors like Sears pledged to withhold contributions, and the President himself threatened travel restrictions and financial retribution if the vote went against his position. Somewhere in the midst of all that, the boycott issues themselves became unimportant and the final vote inevitable.

When Robert Kane, president of the USOC, was asked at the press conference after the vote whether he felt the White House had exerted undue or underhanded pressure on the delegates, he smiled and blushed like an embarrassed schoolboy, searched for words, and finally turned the question over to USOC executive director Don Miller, who, Kane told reporters, was "paid to answer questions like that."

A few people laughed. I felt more at home with embarrassment.

The vote seemed to come, as I said, too easily. It was over. It was time to go home. The decision had been made, and it seemed the easiest decision of the weekend.

I caught a plane out the next morning to Denver and transferred to the Spokane flight. The weather was clear, the scenery was spectacular, and the service was flawless. We even arrived a few minutes ahead of schedule. That day, it seemed, we were sailing with, not against, the wind.

(MAY 1980)

The Sunday Review

I'M SITTING HERE with the Sunday paper. May 25, 1980. On page B4, near the end of the sports section, three remnants of absurd reality stare at me with heartless nonchalance. Without conscience, without tact, and without mercy, they exist on the printed page as the tattered remains of my Olympic dreams.

Sometimes I can stare back at them with equal nonchalance. Sometimes I smile at the irony. Strangely, they do not upset me.

"Sandoval Takes Marathon Trial" is one remnant, a headline in the middle of the page. The article describes how Tony Sandoval won the Olympic Trials Marathon the day before. He is incorrectly described as having been my roommate at Stanford. Though we both attended Stanford, and though we have become good friends over the years, we were not in college at the same time.

The article touches on the situation that has become the benchmark of people's understanding of the relationship between us: the 1976 Trials in Eugene, when we ran close together for over twenty miles, often right next to each other, vying for the third spot on the Olympic team. At somewhere around twenty-three miles I overtook him and went on to capture third.

I crossed the finish line joyously, though my jubilance was touched with the disappointment I saw in Tony's eyes later. It was a bittersweet day.

A scriptwriter's eye would certainly have chosen that day as the beginning scene of the four-year story of Tony Sandoval's quest for a spot on the 1980 Olympic team. The writer might be accused of creating too pat an ending in having Tony win the next Olympic Trials, but otherwise the story would have been good fiction.

I'm not certain how I would have written myself into the story, but as the would-be writer of my own Olympic story, I have been more concerned with my own quest for an Olympic berth.

For four years now, and more intensely in the last twelve months, I've been trying to direct my energies toward the Olympic Trials and Olympic Games. I felt I had a decent chance at performing well in both. At the very least, I thought I would experience the intense excitement of a marathon race in Buffalo, even if the result were the bitter reward of an unsuccessful challenge.

Instead, having heard the marathon results on the telephone Saturday, and then reading them secondhand in the newspaper, I find I have been written out of the Olympic Trials marathon script completely.

A race that was the heart of my plans for four years ended up as an article in the Sunday paper. I read about it as any other sports fan might—as an observer.

A larger headline, above and to the left, signals the reason: "Japanese Go Along." The article, describing the decision of the Japanese Olympic Committee to support a boycott of the Moscow Olympics, is remnant two of the absurd story of my Olympic quest.

A year ago, in defining the obstacles I might face in making the U.S. Olympic team, I never thought to consider a boycott. As it turned out, politics has become the insurmountable obstacle to every American Olympic hopeful.

I wrote earlier of the possible dangers facing anyone with Olympic aspirations: "A rock lies in wait to turn an ankle. A car driver forgets to look to the right as a runner approaches. A muscle in action begins to pull. Billions of viral Rockys look for a body to punch." Conspicuously missing from the litany is the obstacle that has become the biggest of all. Rewriting the list now, I would add, "Hundreds of Soviet tanks roll toward a country to subjugate."

If someone had told me a year ago that I'd better be concerned with the possibility of an Olympic boycott, the suggestion would have seemed ludicrous. Now, with the events of the past six months behind us, the ludicrousness seems to lie in not having foreseen the possibility ahead of time.

The juxtaposition of Sandoval's victory with the report of the latest news in the Olympic boycott makes curious reading indeed. What should have been an athletic achievement with exciting future possibilities is instead a story without an ending. Will Sandoval win a gold medal? The scriptwriter leaves us hanging like an unwitting audience at a theater-of-the-absurd performance. We've been dangling on the edge of our seats in expectation, the hero has made it to step one in magnificent fashion, we're ready for the final act when, suddenly, the curtain closes. End of performance.

Reading this at home, I am mystified by Sandy's comment on his victory: "This is great. Four years ago was heartbreaking." I see no hint of a letdown in his words. No clue that this win might be an even bigger heartbreak than his 1976 loss. There is only the exhilaration of victory, which is, perhaps, as it should be.

Reading this, I feel a certain heartbreak of my own, though, realizing I'll never know if my friend might have won a medal in the 1980 Olympic Games.

The last chapter in my own quest for a spot on the Olympic team should have been written as a participant in the Olympic Trials Marathon in Buffalo. Instead, my interest in running that race began to wane as the likelihood of a boycott grew. When the boycott was finalized in Colorado Springs, I lost interest entirely.

I maintained an interest in competing in other races, possibly the ten thousand meters at the Track and Field Trials in Eugene. I was training well, with some setbacks, when Mother Nature had the final absurd comment on my aspirations. She blew her top.

The third remnant in the newspaper, in the form of advertisements, reveals one of those obstacles every runner should be aware of in preparing for major competition: a volcanic eruption.

"To combat the devastating effects of volcanic ash in your car's engine, officials recommend you change your oil and oil filter every 100 miles.

"Notice: Volcanic ash does not harm two-way radio communications."

On May 18, something happened that almost never happens. A volcano erupted, and Spokane was inundated with fallout. The air swirled with microscopic silicon dust particles, and people were advised to stay indoors. Only a few absolute idiots were outdoors. Naturally, I was one of them.

As the city closed down and the air remained hostile to human lungs, I was one of only a few masked men roaming the streets in running gear. By way of concession to possible health hazards, I cut my training down, and as the emergency situation continued day after day after day, my hopes of regaining racing form in time for the Olympic Track and Field Trials faded.

Mount St. Helens had the final word on my training for the 1980 Olympics.

In a way, the May 25 newspaper is humorous. An Olympic Trials Marathon with no meaning, a boycott that no one foresaw, and Mother Nature's resounding volcanic shout of supremacy. It takes me back a few months to a daydreaming session in the El Rio Restaurant, where I watched hundreds of gnats circling a light outside.

I remember thinking at the time of the parallels between gnats inebriated by a street light and runners inebriated by an Olympic dream. The analogy seemed both humorous and valid.

I went back to the El Rio the other evening, partly to daydream again, but mainly because I was hungry. I hadn't been there in quite a while.

I sat down and looked out the window. The street light was out. I couldn't see the gnats anywhere. Ed, the owner, shouted at me from the bar, "Hey, where have you been?"

As he walked over, I pointed out at the ash-strewn street and answered, "Hiding from this stuff in my basement."

He smiled. "You're not one of these people I see out there running all huddled up in masks, are you?"

"I'm afraid so," I answered.

He shook his head in disgust and walked away. A while later he came back. "You know," he said, "I had to laugh the other day. It was the first day of the ash fallout, and I was listening to the radio.

The announcer called up the EPA guy for Spokane and asked him how the air quality was." Ed let out a laugh. "The guy was horrified. 'It's twenty-five hundred times over normal!' he said. The poor guy couldn't believe it."

I laughed too. Imagine a man working day after day to ensure that the air is clean, to dedicate his life to that goal, only to have something outside his control utterly devastate the effort.

I can empathize. There are a few things you can control in life, but basically, just when you think you've got it figured out—WHAM!

I'm going to throw away that May 25 issue of the paper. That EPA guy and I have the same problem. Reality is just a little too capricious at times. And that's something, as I begin to make training and racing plans for next fall, that I'd rather not be reminded of.

Thirty Phone Booths to Boston

THE PREMARATHON PRESS CONFERENCE was nearly over. Dozens of reporters, almost half of whom seemed to be Japanese, had scattered to the winds, except for a handful who surrounded Billy Rodgers in the hope of eliciting a quote, a look, or even a telltale belch that hadn't already been written down during the typically inane pre-Boston briefing.

A Japanese television company that had traveled thousands of miles to film a full-length version of the 1981 Boston Marathon for prime-time showing back home was wrapping up an interview with Jacqueline Gareau. Caterers were moving tables half-full of coffee and jelly-rolls that had been provided to sweeten the perspectives of the assembled media junkies.

Will Cloney was in good spirits in spite of having endured several weeks of threats to the life of the BAA's annual showcase event. A local township had denied access through their town. The Boston police had vowed to demonstrate against department cutbacks by blocking the race at Cleveland Circle. Will had weathered the various storms in typically unruffled style. Responding to the police challenge a few days earlier, he had told the press, "For many of the runners, Monday's race is the Olympic marathon they were forced to miss last year. To have them disappointed for a second time would be cruel beyond the conscience of any true Greater Bostonian."

The police later voted not to block the course.

In today's conference, Cloney had announced in jest that the last seat on the twelve-passenger lead van was up for grabs to the highest bidder.

"I just had an offer of seventy-eight hundred dollars a few minutes ago," Will quipped. "If anyone is willing to go higher than that, let me know."

I found him later and shoved a twenty-dollar bill his way. "This is for starters," I whispered. "I'll pay you the rest later."

The ploy was unsuccessful. My last-ditch efforts to weasel my way into some sort of position of insight for the eighty-fifth Boston Marathon had failed. One possible spot on the van, one I had thought definite, had vanished a week earlier. By then it was too late to beg myself aboard. And now my attempt to bribe my way into that seat of wisdom with a twenty-dollar bill had fizzled. Twenty bucks wasn't buying what it used to.

Now what? How to cover this thing?

While I pondered the problem, reporters continued to surround Billy like the president's men, and he endured their reverence patiently. After all these years of being Mr. Marathon, the Dalai Lama of the sport is still able to offer sincere and relatively unfettered responses to reporters' questions. He still looks to be the Gee Whiz Kid, surprised to be on stage, honored to be answering questions.

What do you think of your chances?

How good is Seko? Are you afraid of him?

What about the weather?

What about Virgin? Pfeffer? Thomas? Meyer? Kita?

Do you think a woman will ever win the Boston Marathon?

What do you think of Johnny Kelley?

Why do you run?

Et cetera.

Finally, though, Bill offered some sort of justification for having to be on his way, and the group of reporters disbanded. Bill started to leave, but was cornered by a couple of representatives of a marathon in the Philippines, who gave him what looked like rosary beads and a box to store them in, an attempt to woo him to Manila to run.

"That ought to convince him," I thought.

Meanwhile, George Kimball of the Boston *Herald American* came over to where a few of us were standing. His upper body was packed into a blue T-shirt that said, "Slim Whitman Appreciation Society."

"Did you get that when you bought his album collection?" I asked.

"No, a friend gave this to me. He's trying to get me into the society."

"You mean," I asked, "you can't just get in by yourself? You have to have a reference?"

Kimball didn't answer, although he later volunteered that Slim wasn't hitting all the notes so well anymore. "When he gets to the high ones," he said, "he has to have someone yodel for him."

Be that as it may, Kimball had about had it for the day with the marathon. "Let's get out of here," he said to Boston's inveterate and genuinely knowledgeable long-distance chronicler, Tony Reavis.

Reavis declined at first, saying something about wanting to talk to a few of the runners.

"F____ the runners," Kimball responded in good-natured disgust. "Let's go get a Bloody Mary."

And something about that statement, good-natured or not, triggered my response. For good or ill, for this year at least, I had had it with trying to scramble my way onto the lead van with a bunch of sports writers.

"F____ the reporters," I thought. "I'm going back to my room."

It was 11:30 A.M., April twentieth. In thirty minutes the marathon would begin in Hopkinton. My hotel room phone was ringing.

"Well, good morning there, reporter," said the caller. Unmistakably, it was the accent of the South. "Jeff Galloway calling."

"How're you doing this morning, Jeff?"

"Fine. How're y'all doing?"

"Great. What's up?"

"Say, what are you planning on doing for the race? Are you going to watch it on TV?"

"I've got about thirty phone booth numbers here in front of me. I'm going to sit right here in my room and call 'em. If you want to come up and help you're welcome."

It was true. The night before, while the marathoners slept with pasta-filled stomachs, I had driven along the course from Framingham to the Pru, making periodic stops to write down the telephone numbers of key phone booths along the way. The Framingham Railroad Station. Natick Square. Wellesley. Auburndale. Heartbreak Hill. Coolidge Corner. And so on. I would cover this damned encounter between Seko and Rodgers and Catalano and whoever from the comfort of my hotel room, where I had access to Magical Fingers and room service and the telephone. Someone would answer when I called along the course. I was certain of that.

I had a couple of aces in the hole, too, just in case the caper failed. Roy Kissin, who had helped hatch the idea, would call from the start. So would Pat Owens of the New York Road Runners Club. Ned Frederick would be at Wellesley. And of course, if all else failed, there was always the TV.

I got a call from Roy, right on schedule, from Hopkinton a few minutes later.

"The whole place here reeks of liniment and sweat," he reported dutifully. "There's urine on the floor and the walls, and a couple of courteous runners have spit rather awesome oysters on my shoes."

So far, it was sounding like a typical start to a typical marathon.

With the kind of coverage I was expecting to provide, my room was soon filled with eager marathon enthusiasts. There was, however, some skepticism about our chances of keeping up with events. Showing my list of phone booth numbers didn't seem to reduce the level of cynicism. Nor did showing off the extraordinary bird's-eye view of the finish line we had out the hotel window.

"Hey, this is a great view of the finish, isn't it?" said one enthusiast. And then, in feigned surprise, "Hey, you can actually see the finish!"

We watched the start of the race on TV, and since there were no phone booths until the town of Framingham, we had to settle for helicopter shots of the runners for the first five miles or so. Someone was obviously playing the role of rabbit, burning out an early lead. The television showed a tiny speck of red traveling over the rolling hills west of Framingham.

"That's Fanelli," someone in the room said.

"It sure is," someone else added. "Up to his old games."

Ten minutes later the television crew let us know that Gary Fanelli of Pennsylvania was the mysterious rabbit of the race.

Rabbit indeed. I had first met Fanelli at a prerace banquet a few years earlier, when we had spent some time discussing his vegetarianism. At the time, he had seemed extremely serious and intense about things. Especially when I told him that I didn't really enjoy the taste of meat, but that I did enjoy the thought of grinding up animals and eating them. He had stared at me in horror, and I felt ashamed of my joke. Later I would learn of his pranksterism, his love of the Blues Brothers, and his affinity for puns. Now, at the Boston Marathon, he was off to a pace that would bring him through the halfway point in 1:03:10, in an attempt to set up the race for Rodgers or Seko or whoever might want to set a new world mark.

It was about time for the runners to be in Framingham, so I called my first booth. Busy. I called another. No answer. Desperately, I looked in the phone book for the number of a Wendy's hamburger place we had seen along the route the night before. A man answered.

"Can I help you please?"

"Uh, yeah," I answered. "Are you along the marathon course?"

"I beg your pardon?"

"Are you along the marathon course?"

"No, we're not. We're in downtown Boston right across from Filene's."

I was off to a bad start.

By now the runners should have been at eight miles, and I hadn't scored a phone booth yet. I tried a number outside of Natick, at about the eight-mile mark. It rang.

"Hello?"

"Hello," I said. "Who's this?"

"This is Catherine."

"Hello, Catherine. Are you there along the marathon course?"

"Yes." The voice was tentative. "Why?"

"Have the runners gone by there yet?"

"No. Only the wheelchair persons. People."

I convinced Catherine (or was it Katherine?) to wait at the phone until the runners came by. In a minute she was back.

"Number one-twenty is in the lead, and number three is second," she reported. "Then fifteen, then forty-two, then eleven, seven, twenty-seven, forty-nine . . ."

"Okay, that's good," I told her. "Do you know the name of the first one?"

"I don't know," she answered. "All I know is that he was long and tall and skinny."

Fanelli.

Catherine agreed to wait at the phone until the women came by. When I called her back in a few minutes, though, the voice sounded a little different.

"Is this Catherine?" I asked.

"No, this is Karyn. I'm her sis-tuh."

"Oh, okay. Have the women come by there yet, Karyn?"

"No, not yet."

"Okay. Well, let me know."

A couple of minutes passed, and Karyn reported that a van with TV cameras had just gone by. I advised her that the first woman should be close behind.

"There she is. From North Carolina. Julie Shea."

About twenty seconds later, number two, Patti Catalano, passed Karyn's phone booth, followed shortly by Joan Benoit.

"Thanks for your help, Karyn," I said.

"What magazine is this for?" she asked.

"*Running* magazine," I answered, and for some reason I felt compelled to spell it. "R-U-N-N-I-N-G."

I seemed to be hitting my stride now, so as soon as I hung up I called the next phone number right away, a booth at Natick Square, just past the ten-mile point. A man answered and identified himself as Tom.

"Tom," I said, "have the lead runners come by there yet?"

"Yeah, they just came by."

"Who was in the lead?"

"I don't know. Just a second." There was a pause while Tom checked with his friends. "Oh. It was a cop. A motorcycle."

A few seconds passed, and Tom gave a second report. "Number one-twenty was in the lead. Farelli [*sic*]."

"Fanelli?"

"Yeah, right."

"Did he look tired at all?"

"No, not at all. He's a big tall guy. He had long, tall strides."

"How about the second guy?"

"He's a short guy."

Tom also agreed to wait to see who the first woman runner would be. Meanwhile, I asked him a little about himself. After all, a writer has to know his sources.

"Have you ever run yourself, Tom?"

"Nah, I've never run the marathon. I would have liked to, but I can't seem to get the time or energy. No spunk, I guess."

"Do you watch this race every year?"

"Oh, yeah. Every year."

"Are you a Bill Rodgers fan?"

"Yeah, we're all rooting for him. And we'll be rooting for the Red Sox this afternoon."

A few minutes passed.

"There's a big cheer now," Tom reported. "That might be the first girl." Pause. "There she goes. I didn't catch her number, though."

"Did she have dark hair?"

"No, she was tall with brown hair."

I thanked him and hung up. Putting together the information from television and the phone booth at Natick, it appeared that Julie Shea was leading, followed by Patti Catalano, Allison Roe, and Jackie Gareau. I placed my next call to Wellesley Square.

"Hello?"

"Hello," I said, "have the runners come by there yet?"

"Yes, they have."

"Who's this?" I asked.

"This is Peter? Who's this?"

"This is Don Kardong. I'm covering this for *Running* magazine. How'd the runners look to you when they came by?"

"They looked real good. Fanelli was in the lead by about a hundred yards, and then number six, Kirk Pfeffer, out of Thousand Oaks."

"Great. By the way, where are you located?"

"I'm right down the street from Wellesley College."

"Can you see the scene at the college from there? Are the girls screaming?"

"Oh, yeah. It's wild there."

The first women runners had already gone by, and Peter reported that Patti Catalano was leading, followed by Jackie Gareau. I thanked him and hung up. My next call, a sure thing, was to the Nike store at Wellesley, where Ned Frederick had promised to file a report. I soon had him on the line. "Hey, listen," Ned told me, "the eating level here is really high. There's some intense eating going on. A lot of beer-drinking, too. People are throwing down three or four at a time."

"Into the street?"

"Yeah, everywhere."

Indeed. I was to learn later that Garry Bjorklund, only semifit for this year's race, would spot a friend at Wellesley who was drinking a beer and holding out a sponge for him. Garry would stop, take the friend's beer, and call it quits for the day.

Ned agreed to go back to the street, watch the leaders go by, then return to the phone. In about five minutes he was back.

"Don?"

"Yeah?"

"They just went past. Fanelli is in the lead, but not for much longer. It looked like he was sort of blacking out. He was blinking and looking down a lot. He had his arms up. He really looked tight."

"How about the other runners?"

"Rodgers is leading that second pack, followed by Seko and Kita. Rodgers looks real good."

"Better than Seko?"

Ned laughed. "No. Seko and Kita were handing water back and forth, kind of joking with each other."

"Well, you know how those Japanese are," I said. "Never a straight man."

"Right," Ned laughed. "Oh, and Virgin didn't look too good. He was right in that first group, but he had that frown on his face. It's hard to tell, though. He always looks like that."

I flashed back to a conversation I had had with Craig two days earlier. He had talked about strategy, about staying with Rodgers and Seko, about the uncertainty of the marathon, about having been "beaten up by the marathon" in Fukuoka. Now, at fifteen miles, he was within striking distance. Was he in trouble or not?

"Ned," I asked, "how much of a lead does Fanelli have there?"

"About nine or ten seconds is all. But he looks really terrible. I give him another two miles, maximum."

"All those carrots and lettuce are failing him at this point."

"Yeah, right."

The rabbit was fading, but at fifteen miles he had set up one hell of a race.

Marci's Restaurant, about one mile farther down the line, was next on my list.

"Is Marci there?" I asked the woman who answered.

"Who's calling?"

"This is Don Kardong with *Running* magazine. I want to see if I can get an update on the runners coming by the restaurant there."

There was a pause.

"All right," the woman said at last. "Hold on."

A minute passed.

"You want an update?" Marci said, picking up the phone, obviously in good humor. "I'm the winner!"

"You're the winner?" I replied. "What's your name? I'll need it for my article."

"It's Marci Hanes."

"Marci, this is Don Kardong from *Running* magazine. Can you give me some information on how things are going there at Marci's Restaurant?"

"Oh, it's going soop-uh."

"Do you have a lot of people outside waiting for the runners to go by?"

"They just went by. The leaders did."

"How'd they look?"

"Good!"

"How about the guy in the lead there. Did he look like he was fading, or did he look strong?"

"He looked pretty strong to us as he went by. But of course the others weren't far behind him."

"Did you offer him anything to eat or drink there at the restaurant?"

"He went by too fast."

I thanked Marci, hung up, and called a booth outside of Newton-Wellesley Hospital, near the seventeen-mile mark, where I had dropped out of the 1979 race with leg cramps. A woman answered.

"Hello?"

"Hello," I answered. "Who's this?"

"Oh. Well, who do you want?"

"I'm trying to get an update on the marathon runners. I'm with *Running* magazine out of Eugene, Oregon."

"From Ory-gone! Oh, my goodness."

As it turned out, the lady I was talking to was waiting for her son Harvey from Harvard to come by. In the meantime, she gave me some information on the race.

"The gentleman who was leading, some unheard-of guy, Falelli or something, is still up front. He has maybe a hundred-foot lead. Bill Rodgers is with a group of eight or ten others right behind, and he looks good."

Between the hospital and the next phone booth, just past eighteen miles, things changed drastically. I spoke with a man named Mike, who, as it turned out, was helping report for the radio pool. The lead runners were just approaching the booth.

"Seventeen, twenty-two," he reported. Grey Meyer had taken the lead, followed by Chettle of Australia and Seko. "Twenty-four, seven, one-twenty." Malcolm East, Kyle Heffner, and Fanelli. Mike couldn't see Rodgers.

I hung up and called back to Marci for an update on the women's race. Marci reported that Patti Catalano had taken over from Julie Shea and that Jackie Gareau was in third. It wasn't clear who was in second place. Maybe Shea, maybe Allison Roe.

The lead runners were now into the set of hills that climaxes, at about twenty-two miles, with Heartbreak Hill. I called the number of a booth just past the wall. Just past twenty miles.

"Hello?"

"Hello, who's this?"

"You're calling Commonwealth Avenue. This is a public phone."

"Right. I'm doing a report for *Running* magazine. Have the lead runners come by there yet?"

"They should be about a minute away."

"Okay. Were you just standing there by the phone," I asked, "or did you want to use it?"

"I was just standing here." Minding my own business, he might have added.

"Okay, good. Say, would you mind giving me your impressions on how the lead runners look when they come by? Who actually looks, in the face, like he's going to win."

Pause.

"I'll give it a try."

The man, whose name was John, turned out to be a longtime resident of the area who watches the marathon pass through his neighborhood every year. As I waited, I could hear helicopters, police cars, and then the rising cheers of the crowd.

According to John's reading of the situation, Rodgers was somewhere around tenth place, but not far behind Seko, the leader.

"The front runners all looked pretty relaxed," he said after the group had passed. "Rodgers looked like he was working the hardest."

As the leaders challenged the hills, the race was beginning to shape up as a battle between Seko, Virgin, and Rodgers, with Rodgers clearly in trouble. I looked at my list of numbers, found one at the thirty-five-kilometer mark, and punched the numbers. The phone rang over and over again. Finally a woman answered.

"Hello?"

"Hello, this is Don Kardong from *Running* magazine. Have the runners come by there yet?"

Hysterical laughter. Then finally, "No, just the wheelchairs."

"Would you mind watching the runners when they come by and letting me know who looks the best?"

"Oh."

"It'll be Craig Virgin in yellow, and the Japanese runner, Seko, in white."

"Do I just leave you here?"

"Just leave the phone hanging."

She laughed. "We were debating for twenty minutes whether to answer the phone or not."

"Oh, yeah? How come you answered it?"

"I don't know. I just thought the hell with it."

The voice on the other end belonged to Caroline Conley, who was watching for some friends of hers to pass. She returned to the phone after a minute or two. "Bill Rodgers just went by," she said.

"How does he look?"

"He's pretty far behind. I don't know. He looks strong. The other two, Virgin and Seko, are neck and neck. Rodgers is a full fifteen or twenty seconds behind, but he looks great!"

"What would your bet be between those first two, Virgin and Seko?"

"I think Seko's going to do it. He didn't even look like he was breathing hard. The other guy looked sweaty and tired."

"Okay, thanks."

"Hey, wait a minute. What's your name?"

"My name? Don Kardong."

"Well, the friends we're waiting for—actually there are three of them, Kevin, Kenny and Jeff—are going to be running from New York to Boston next month to raise money for a disease that Kevin's daughter has."

"What's the disease?"

"Tuberous sclerosis. Anyone who wants to help out can send contributions to the Tuberous Sclerosis Foundation in Carver, Mass. They know about the run there and they'd be the people to get in touch with. Can you spell your last name again?"

I spelled my name, promised to send money, hung up, and called the Bill Rodgers Running Center at Cleveland Circle, at about twenty-two miles. Not surprisingly, there was no answer. But if I had known, I could have gotten a good race report by calling one of a number of top runners who had dropped out or failed to enter this year's Boston race, preferring instead to watch TV and play the video machines at Chip's, a bar down the street from Rodgers's store.

Mike Roche, who had had his foot stomped by a police horse while watching for the lead runners at Cleveland Circle, had screamed in pain and hopped across to Chip's in search of ice. Garry Bjorklund, after quitting at Wellesley, was now scoring well at Space Invaders.

Not knowing they were available for update duty, I called instead to a booth somewhere between twenty-three and twenty-four miles. A girl answered.

"Hi," I said. "This is Don Kardong with *Running* magazine. Can you give me an update on the race?"

There was no hesitation. The girl, whose name was Paula, told me the runners had already come by.

"The first guy, the Chinese guy, probably came by about forty-five seconds ago. Virgin is about twenty yards behind him."

"How's Billy doing?"

"Oh, he's pretty far behind. He's got a lot of catching up to do."

I called back quickly to Caroline at 35K and found that the women had just passed.

"W2 just went by," she said. "Is that Patti Catalano?"

"Right."

"She was running with a group of guys. And there was a van next to her. It looked like a Japanese film crew."

"They're filming the women's race," I told her. "How did Patti look?"

"She looked pretty strong. There was another woman not that far behind her, a blonde, number W8. She was only two or three seconds behind."

And that was the first clear indication I had of the upset-in-the-making for Allison Roe of New Zealand. I had caught a glimpse, through the magic of phone-booth reporting, of almost the exact instant she made her move on Patti, a move that would bring her to a resounding Boston victory.

Time was running out on the men's race, so I called the phone number of writer Ray Krise at Hereford Street, only a few hundred yards from the finish.

"The wheelchairs just went by," Ray told me. "The top three were all within two minutes of each other, with Bob Hall in third. He's a personal friend of mine, so he's the guy I was looking for most. Curt Brinkman just went by in fourth. Number four, Jim Martinsen, was first, from Washington. I'm not even going to try to pronounce the name of the city he's from. You'd probably do a lot better than I would."

"It's Puyallup, Ray. By the way, where exactly are you located there?"

"I'm at the corner of Newbury and Hereford Street, a hundred yards from the Pru. We've got three cases of beer in the fridge, and half the people I'm expecting are still trying to find parking. Coach Bill Squires has officially recognized this apartment as the best place in the world to watch the Boston Marathon from. Why don't you guys come on over and get drunk?"

"Sounds great, Ray. See you in a bit."

Back in the room, we had shifted our attention from the television to the scene out the window, in anticipation of Seko's finish. It was clear at that point that, barring a confrontation with a Boston Police horse, nothing was going to prevent him from securing the victory he had been planning for months. Seko's intense hill training, three weeks of acclimatization in Boston, and the protection of his coach from the ravages of the media had provided the strength necessary for his triumph. Now, outside the hotel, helicopters swarmed in expectation of his victory, while hundreds of spectators ran across the roof of the Sheraton to watch Seko's final steps along Boylston Street.

After what seemed like an unnaturally long run down the final stretch, Toshihiko Seko broke the tape at 2:09:26, one second better that Rodgers's previous Boston record.

Rodgers seemed to have closed the gap some on Virgin, but Craig held on for a 2:10:26, eight seconds ahead of a teeth-gritting Rodgers. John Lodwick and Malcolm East finished fourth and fifth a minute later, clocking 2:11:33 and 2:11:35. Greg Meyer, who had led at eighteen miles, was eleventh at 2:13:07, and the rabbit, Gary Fanelli, cruised in at 2:22:25, just making the top hundred. It was a day made for racing, as nearly three hundred runners slid in under two-and-a-half hours.

I thought I might be able to catch the latest development in the women's race, so I called one of a set of four booths at a little past twenty-five miles.

"Have the women come by there yet?" I asked the woman who answered.

"No. Nobody here," she replied.

It sounded like I had reached a wrong number, so I called another of the set of four. The same woman answered.

"Is this the same number I just called?"

"Yah, but this is a public telephone."

"Isn't this a phone booth along the marathon course?"

"No, no, sorry," she replied, laughing.

Whether it was or wasn't (and of course it was), it was clear I wasn't going to get much of an update from her. I hung up and called Coolidge Corner, the twenty-four-mile mark. A man answered.

"Have the women gone by yet?"

"Yeah, two."

"Was Patti in the lead?"

"No, she was second, probably twenty yards behind."

"The blonde?"

"She was in first."

It still hadn't been reported on TV yet, but it seemed clear that

Allison Roe was about to seal her upset victory. While we watched Seko and Rodgers being interviewed, my phone rang. I was hoping it might be any one of several people who had offered to phone in reports.

"Hello," a woman said. "Do you need maid service today?"

That call signaled the end of my telephone escapade. I decided to quit letting my fingers do the running, sit back, and join the crew watching TV. In a few minutes, Allison Roe crossed the line in 2:26:46, as close as anyone has come to joining Grete Waitz's class of female marathon runner. She was whisked through the crowd by two police, one on each arm.

"Hey!" Jeff Galloway said in mock horror. "They're taking her away!"

"They're searching her for subway tokens," said erstwhile *Running* magazine publisher Jack Welch, who had been making similar comments for over two hours.

Next came Patti Catalano, setting a new American record of 2:27:51, yet obviously upset at having to play the bridesmaid at Boston for the third straight year. She was followed by Joan Benoit (2:30:16), early leader Julie Shea (2:30:54), and last year's Boston winner, Jackie Gareau (2:31:26).

We all enjoyed a few minutes of the Allison Roe conference, but there's something about hearing a beautiful blonde Kiwi talk about "undulating terrain" that makes one not want to sit in one place for too long. We decided to accept Ray Krise's invitation to join the crowd at his place on Hereford Street.

A few minutes later we were in an apartment that is deemed "the best road-racing apartment in the U.S." and "the best place in the world to watch the Boston Marathon, according to Bill Squires." The latter was certainly true, as we found out by standing on the fire escape, where we could overlook the hundreds of Boston marathoners as they made their way over the last few paces of the course.

Ray did, as promised, have a fridge full of beer, and before long our enthusiasm over the various runners finishing reached fever pitch. We greeted George Sheehan as he passed without a shirt, and Jim

Fixx as he finished without a smile. We watched the winners of various divisions that Jack Welch invented on the spot.

"There's the first finisher in black high-tops!" Jack yelled. "There's the first sweater finisher! There's the first finisher in fluorescent shoes! There's the first hoodlum! The first illegal alien! The first Halloween finisher!" And on and on in descending levels of absurdity.

We watched from the fire escape as Jack identified the gold, silver, and bronze medalists in the punk division, the latter with curly hair, a long-sleeved striped shirt, dark glasses, and red high-tops. The man was also second in the high-top division. We watched the gold medalist in the women's punk division run by dressed entirely in green, including, of course, her face and hair.

We also watched and yelled for everyone who had their names on their shirts: Paul, Tricia, Barbara, Super Sue, Carol, Harold, Pat, Marty, Rocky, and the Havliceks (Muriel and Ed). Our chants of "Fred! Fred! Fred!" usually brought some sort of tired response from the identified runner, and a chant of "Pretzel! Pretzel! Pretzel!" to the local vender below actually resulted in a couple of the salty biscuits flying our way. Free of charge.

When we didn't have a name to yell, we yelled whatever was on the runner's T-shirt. "No Nukes! No Nukes! No Nukes!" and "Small Is Beautiful! Small Is Beautiful! Small Is Beautiful!" and "Save the Whales! Save the Whales! Save the Whales!" and "Oregon! Oregon! Oregon!" and "Free the Shah! Free the Shah! Free the Shah!" and "Spam! Spam! Spam!" Finally, when someone on the fire escape asked us, "What magazine did you guys say you were from?" we decided the fun was over.

It was about time anyway. Johnny Kelley was coming by, flanked by two motorcycles and dozens of runners. After he had passed to the thunder of the crowd's appreciation, everyone began to leave. Police protection ended at four hours. The cool weather became light snowfall, and the wind was blowing harder. The last runners passed below us amid swirling trash and horse apples.

Thus ended my Boston Marathon. It was the first one I had

followed by calling telephone booths along the way, and the gambit provided excellent coverage by on-the-spot reporters Catherine, Karyn, Tom, Peter, Marci, Ned, Mike, John, Caroline, Paula, Ray, Roy, and a few others. Generally, they gave better coverage than the networks.

When it was all over, when we were watching those last few bandits finishing their twenty-six miles below, I realized what a great day it had been. Excellent conditions, exciting racing, and the joy of screaming our inebriated heads off from Ray's fire escape in raucous encouragement for the vast parade of Boston Marathon finishers. It was the most fun I've ever had at a Boston race.

Next year, though, I don't intend to fly all the way to Boston just to follow the damned race by calling phone booth numbers from my hotel room. After all, I've still got those numbers, and I've got a phone in my bedroom. Next year, I won't have to fly to Boston at all.

Grete Waitz —
New York 1980

WE SAT, we sprawled, we huddled in the room for invited runners at Fort Wadsworth, waiting for the start of the New York City Marathon.

Outside, the wind gusted above thirty miles an hour. It had blown down the runners' tent shelter and knocked over the world's largest urinal. Fourteen thousand runners cowered behind bushes, under blankets, and inside garbage bags, hoarding their warmth while they waited for the race to start.

In the invited-runners' quarters there was very little noise. Some quiet discussions, a flurry of excited greetings from Patti Lyons-Catalano to everyone when she entered, then more subdued quiet.

Suddenly, so it seemed, the Finns, led by Lasse Viren, were up in the middle of the room, rubbing some sort of ointment on their legs. The powerful analgesic scent brought back memories of high school cross-country meets, when we used the lotion in liberal quantities before races. I hadn't used it since, nor, I suspected, had most of the other runners in the room. Everyone stared in rapt attention.

After a minute or two, a few other runners followed the Finnish lead. They began borrowing dabs of analgesic and rubbing it on with grim determination.

By now the Finns were down to jockstraps, and the analgesic balm was being applied to arms, torso, and buttocks. It didn't take long for the rest of us to be drawn in. In a few minutes the entire room was alive with runners rubbing themselves with analgesic. Lasse looked up, noticed the result of the Finnish example, and said something in his native tongue to Eino Romppanen, a Finnish-born American in the room.

Eino nodded. "Lasse says," he announced to us all, "that he's rubbing on reindeer shit."

And to emphasize the point, he added on his own, "That's Lasse's secret—reindeer shit."

To my left, Grete Waitz stood, several large dabs of liniment punctuating her thighs. She rubbed the stuff in. Even Grete had been caught up in the analgesic mystique.

Even Grete. The phrase suggests the uniqueness of the individual, the uniqueness of her excellence among female distance runners. Twice she had run the New York City Marathon. Twice she had set the women's world record on the difficult New York course.

She had never lost a marathon. Or a road race. Or a cross-country race. No other woman had run under 2:30 before.

She has been to women's distance running what Viren has been to men's. And now she stood rubbing Lasse's secret into her legs, preparing for a cold day in New York.

"Have you used that before?" I asked.

One day she may learn to lead reporters on, the way Lasse does. To lead them around in circles of reindeer and blood-doping and Nordic nonsense when they search for the secret. For now, though, she answered simply and truthfully.

"Yes, when it's cold."

I was searching for the secret, too, or at least the essence, of Grete's astounding successes. I hadn't told her so, for fear of upsetting her race plan, but as she attacked the New York streets in her third marathon, I would be tracking her, trying to learn how it was that Grete always managed to humiliate the roads she traveled.

There were many questions on my mind.

Would this be the day Patti Lyons-Catalano would seriously challenge her friend and athletic foe, Grete Waitz? I had spoken with her the day before, and she seemed fit and eager for a good race. Having set American records on the roads at every distance from five miles through the marathon during the preceding months, she seemed a likely bet to oust Grete as Marathon Queen that day, if anyone was a likely bet.

What about the weather? Was the wind going to help or hinder performances? At a press conference Saturday, while gusts of wind and rain pounded the windowpanes behind him, Alberto Salazar had come as close as he ever would to retracting his predicted first-marathon time of 2:10.

"I want to set the record straight on that. What I meant to say was that if someone else runs 2:10, I'll run 2:10."

Thus did Alberto make a slight bow of courtesy to the New York City monsoon.

And what about my own performance? How easy was it going to be to run Grete's pace? I considered the likelihood of dropping off a fast pace and hobbling home to Central Park, without dignity and without a story. I didn't like the image at all.

I began rubbing more reindeer droppings on my thighs and calves.

Fifteen minutes before race time, I was still undecided about one thing. Should I start on the women's side near Grete, or on the men's side as the color of my number suggested?

I had gotten permission to start with the women, which would be the surest way of keeping Grete in sight, but something about trying to link up with the lead group of females after three miles of divided running was intriguing. I was torn between the two starting positions.

I imagined myself on the women's line, six inches taller than anyone else, showing up clearly in all the pictures. That was not a photo my friends would let me forget. The image sent me straight to the men's section on the Verrazano Bridge.

The cannon shot beginning the marathon was deafening, prompting the horde of runners to take off like . . . well, like frightened reindeer, I suppose. We stampeded down the road, trying to avoid a good trampling.

A strong wind was at our backs, the New York skyline was ahead, and the cannon shot seemed to have opened a nest of helicopters above. Everywhere the buzz of blades.

My own thoughts were on the projected link-up with the women's field in a few more miles. Was I running the right speed? Five-twenty pace seemed about right, but I passed the mile marker at 5:30. I picked up the pace slightly.

Suddenly a piece of yellow paper blew by. I looked over at the guy running next to me.

"There's nothing I hate more," I told him, "than getting passed by a piece of paper."

"Don't worry about it," he returned. "He can't hold it for the distance. He'll crumple at twenty miles."

We came off the bridge and turned onto Ninety-second Street, and in a minute or two we spotted the first runners from the other section. Photograph fiends, no doubt, sprinting madly to get their pictures in the *New York Times*. The actual lead runners, the top women, were likely close behind.

I followed other runners onto Fourth Avenue and looked behind to my left. I thought I could see the women's group a short distance back, so I slowed down. In a few seconds Joe Catalano pulled up next to me.

"Where's Patti?" I asked him.

"Right behind us."

And there they ran, accompanied by several dozen male runners: Patti, Grete, and Ingrid Kristiansen, Grete's Norwegian teammate.

One must wonder at the pack of males who ran with Grete and Patti through most of the race. There were at least two reporters I know of in the group, myself and Amby Burfoot, and for a while Joe Catalano ran there as well. But who were the rest? The guy on Grete's left who offered her drinks at every aid station? The guy on her right who offered to shelter her from the wind? The guy who ran two paces ahead for miles and miles?

Responding to some kind of male protective instinct perhaps, or to a desire to be part of the phenomenon of Grete's running ability, or maybe just caught up in the electricity surrounding the women's race, they hovered around her like the queen's court, following her from the very beginning through all five boroughs of New York City, until Grete finally left them all panting in the park, victims of her awesome speed.

True to her queenly bearing, Grete seldom acknowledged their offers of assistance, used them as shelter from the wind, or married her own pace to theirs.

One thing is clear. Grete needs no one's help to break records. The men follow her, not vice versa. From start to finish she stares straight ahead, seeming to focus her concentration on a distant finish line, noticing no one around her.

I was amused to hear her answer to the question, "How long was Patti Catalano with you?" at the press conference following the marathon. I was amused not just because Grete's answer of "Eight or nine miles" was way off, but mainly because, from start to finish, she never turned to see who was with her. How could she possibly guess the duration of Patti's marathon companionship? The woman, quite simply, does not look back.

Patti's own account of the separation of the two is more to the point. Hearing a five-mile split of 27:03, she decided the early pace might spell disaster later on. It was good-bye, Grete, at that point. See you at the finish.

Having raced the first five miles at a pace suggesting a 2:22 marathon, Grete was now all alone. Except, of course, for the gaggle of male runners, which included fifty-year-old Piet Van Alphen of Holland, a 2:22 racer himself. Piet settled in next to Grete, where he ran for the next ten or twelve miles.

From five to ten miles, Grete's pace slowed from 5:24 to around 5:34 per mile. As the crowd along Brooklyn's Fourth Avenue watched the runners cruise by, they noticed Grete among the field.

"Is that Grete? That's Grete, isn't it? That is! That's Grete Waitz!"

"Atta girl! Go get 'em!"

"You're the foist goil!"

"She's not a girl, she's a woman."

"Go, Grete, go!"

"Go, babe, you can do it!"

"Hey, there's the first chick!"

"Yay, ERA!"

"Gret-uh! Gret-uh! Gret-uh!"

"Yaaaaaaaaaayyyyyyyyyyyy!"

The men watching were appreciative, no doubt, but the women spectators went bonzo. The many images of females responding to Grete's passage along the course merge in my mind into a single image of a screaming, smiling, cheering, shouting, multiracial woman waving both arms and jumping up and down in glee, emitting sounds that cannot be spelled.

They love Grete in New York.

Reindeer shit or no reindeer shit, it was bound to happen. After passing ten miles in 54:53 (projecting a 2:24 marathon), after cruising through a cluster of Hasidic Jews, and before reaching the marathon's halfway point, we passed Lasse Viren. There was no photographer to chronicle the eclipsing of the best male Olympic distance runner of all time by the fastest female distance runner of all time. It happened quickly, quietly, graciously.

Lasse, out of shape for this event, had announced his impending retirement before the race. Shortly after we passed, he retired from the New York City Marathon and from active competition in general.

It happens.

Grete surged through the last bit of Brooklyn and onto the Pulaski Bridge. Her group of followers spread out a bit, thinned by the wind and the rising slope of the bridge. She passed the halfway point. 1:12:37. The woman who claimed she was racing for victory, not records, was on line for a 2:25:12, a time that would best her current world record by well over two minutes.

Off the Pulaski Bridge and through Queens, Grete's pace continued at around 5:35. Her group of escorts had now dwindled to a half-dozen or so, some of them moving slightly ahead, some behind.

The crowd's excitement had been continuous since we first entered Brooklyn, but as we ran up to the Queensboro Bridge, the noise faded. There were officials scattered across the span, but no spectators.

On the left, the Manhattan skyline stood impressively. From the left, the wind gusted without mercy. Shunning the protection of the male runners around her, Grete forged ahead, and all of us were buffeted continually, sometimes nearly tripping over the metal divider on the inside.

Aside from the wind's pounding, though, the Queensboro Bridge was a quiet interlude in the race. As we ran across toward Manhattan, the skyline seemed inviting. This could almost have been a New York training run among friends. Except for the pace.

We came off the bridge onto First Avenue, and the Manhattan crowd exploded. Grete had arrived, they knew it, and they let her know it. Jack Waitz, Grete's husband, rushed out to meet her as she passed sixteen miles, shouting words of encouragement that Grete could only dimly hear. Jack's presence nevertheless seemed to give her a lift as she began her triumphant journey along First Avenue.

After the race, Grete would be asked how she felt about the New York crowd's enthusiasm for her.

"New York is like a second home for me," she replied, smiling.

Some home. The crowd on First Avenue was overwhelming. It's easy to speak of being moved to tears, but it's not an easy thing to experience in the middle of a marathon. I was surprised at my own emotional reaction to the uproar.

The response of the crowd, their enthusiastic endorsement of Grete's athletic skill, was electrifying and emotionally devastating. At the time, I wondered whether the energy generated was a help or a hindrance to her. If figures can be trusted, her pace along the Avenue slowed to 5:45. But whether she slowed down or not, it was deeply moving and humanly reassuring to witness the ticker-tape response to the best female runner in the world.

Perhaps it hit a familiar chord in my own racing past, reminding me of one or two times when a large crowd cheered me on during a race. Nostalgic eyewash, I suppose, and I was glad when we finally left most of the First Avenue crowd behind and could concentrate again on the marathon itself.

At the end of First Avenue, where folks had hung a sign saying 19½ MILES—THE HARLEM WALL, we crossed the Willis Avenue Bridge

and headed into the Bronx. For the first time during the entire race,
I heard a shout out of running's distant past.

"You're not going to let a girl beat you, are you?"

Two or three years ago, this might have been everyman's favorite
taunt. It is a measure of Grete's greatness, of her influence on changing attitudes, and of her overall recognition among a New York
crowd of marathon sophisticates that the taunt no longer seemed
interesting.

When Grete Waitz passes Lasse Viren in a race, who can look
the other way, pretending that women haven't earned a place of
respect in the world of athletics?

Next year in this marathon, maybe no one will yell, "Hey, you're
not going to let a girl beat you, are you?"

Grete passed twenty miles at 1:51:23, an average of 5:34, en
route to a 2:26 marathon. The trick of the New York City Marathon,
though, is that the course gets tougher as the legs get weaker. That
2:26 wasn't guaranteed. At just past twenty-one miles we made a
final bridge crossing and headed up Fifth Avenue into the wind.

Grete's pigtail blew horizontally, and she almost stopped as the
wind gusted repeatedly. In spite of this, she managed to stay close
to her target pace. The record that she claimed not to want was
within her reach.

By this point in the race, the rolling hills and gusting wind had
withered most of her entourage. As she entered Central Park at
twenty-four miles, she was the only leaf left on the tree, with the
possible exception of this reporter, who was hanging on to the branch
for dear life.

Grete, as she will tell you, is a track runner, not a marathoner.
To prove that point, she began a startling race through Central Park
to the finish. As she passed the flotsam and jetsam of the men's race,
her strength, speed, and determination spoke a story different from
theirs: her face, strained but eager; their faces, drained of hope.

At about twenty-five miles, Jack again came onto the course,
encouraging Grete's sprint. She had just run the twenty-fifth mile
in 5:13. On the digital clock at that point the time read 2:19:18.

The mad dash continued around the south end of the park, past spectators and lagging runners. Visions of Karel Lismont floated to mind. Grete ticked off another 5:13 on the twenty-sixth mile and sprinted the spare change to the finish.

I punched my watch as she crossed. 2:25:41.

As I crossed the line myself, announcer Tony Reavis said, "Don, Grete beat you again."

Make that only *two* times in the 1980 New York City Marathon that anyone spoke of girls beating boys.

The 1980 New York City Marathon was won in record time by a man who believes the marathon is just another distance race. Nothing unusual. Nothing sacred. A lot easier than some ten-kilometer races he's run.

The women's winner, Grete Waitz, ran start to finish without once glancing behind her to notice who was there. I ran undiscovered. The world record is unimportant to her, although her time of 2:25:41 would have won half the men's Olympic marathons in history. She's a track racer.

In the psychological slipstream created by Grete, Patti Lyons-Catalano, who stopped smoking and drinking a few years ago to become an athlete, became the second-fastest female marathoner of all time. The fastest American woman ever.

Bob Dylan, who has never run the marathon, who does not even own a pair of running shoes, and who scorns the excrement of reindeer, nevertheless summed up the race nicely.

"The times, they are a-changin'."

Ten years ago, not one woman finished the New York City Marathon. In 1980, about two thousand finished, and only two spectators made comments about girls beating boys.

That, fellow runners, is what I call progress.

"Ladies and gentlemen, boys and girls, step right this way for the wonder-drug of the decade. Made from lowly droppings of the princely reindeer, it is the Scandinavian secret of running success. Lasse's lotion. Grete's gift. You, too, can run with the stars. Step right this way. . . ."

Alberto Salazar, 1982

It's almost impossible for me to imagine anyone but Alberto Salazar winning the 1982 New York City Marathon. The confidence, the brashness, the brazen assurance of the man have warped my powers of imagining.

If he were a salesman, I would have bought the Edsel. Or the swampland in Florida. Or the Brooklyn Bridge. Not from slick talking, but from the sheer certainty emanating from him. Two days before the big race, a few seconds before landing in New York to watch him live up to his expectations, I am still enveloped in that confidence. Though it's dark outside, I can still see almost the entire marathon course below, and I can imagine the race developing only one way: Salazar, amid a slowly dwindling pack of contenders, cranking out mile after blazing mile, finally running alone in the streets of the Big Apple.

Try as I might, I can't visualize him dropping off the pace, abandoning victory in the New York streets below.

FLASHBACK: OCTOBER 5, 1982   *The Salazar Residence*

"I'm rapidly getting to the point now where I don't care about interviews or anything anymore," says Alberto Salazar, at home in Eugene. "I guess from a business point of view every bit of publicity you can get is good, but it's just not worth it to me. You get sick of talking about the same thing over and over again."

No one said interviewing him would be easy.

The mood hasn't been uneasy but the answers have been quick, to the point, and generally uninspired. I'm searching for a clue to this man who stood the running world on its ear by winning his first marathon in 2:09:41 and setting a world record in his second. I'm looking for the previously undiscovered personality trait, hidden under some unturned rock of dialogue. Instead, I only seem to be asking questions he's heard before, and hearing answers that lead nowhere.

Well, not nowhere. Only to the same conclusion. The straightforward answer. That Salazar has developed confidence based on exceptional training. That he, with Coach Bill Dellinger's assistance, has analyzed himself and his opponents, and organized a training schedule designed to place him at the front of the pack. Training schedule adhered to, conclusion obvious. Victory at New York.

"I feel I'm a better runner than I was last year. Stronger, faster. I think I'm in a minute better shape, at least. I'm prepared to go through the half-marathon in 1:03."

One-oh-three.

A statement like that may seem pretentious, cocky, outrageous. Salazar, though, has never been one to hide his feelings, whether those feelings relate to his fellow runners or his own abilities.

"I guess I *am* more blunt than the average person," he says simply.

But the prediction of victory, the analysis of his own ability, and the absence of braggadocio when he considers a 1:03 first half are all supportable with hard data. In 1981, Salazar ran 27:40 for ten thousand meters on the track; in 1982, he set an American record of 27:25.6. This summer he also set the American record at five thousand meters (13:11.9) and ran a new course record at the highly competitive Falmouth Road Race. Clearly, he's in the best racing condition of his life.

Kenny Moore has pointed to Salazar's family history and Latin pride in explaining Alberto's success. As Salazar analyzes his own abilities, though, I sense more the cold logic of systematic training and undisputed results.

He isn't especially excited to describe his training. Not to hide a secret, but rather to avoid belaboring the obvious. Stress and rest.

Mileage and intervals. Heal the injuries, strengthen the weaknesses. The end point, then, is predictable.

"I don't feel there's anything anybody can do in there that I can't. I feel I've got the speed on everybody that's in the race. By that I'm not necessarily saying hundred-meter sprint speed."

Salazar laughs, his brown eyes twinkling. Undisputably, he is not a hundred-meter man. He knows that no amount of pride can change that fact.

"What I'm saying is that I could beat 'em all at the five thousand, so if I wanted to I could wait until the last three miles. And I feel I've got as much or more strength than any of them. Surging, uneven pace—I've done that. So I don't feel there's anything I have to worry about from another runner. I'm just basically trying to get myself in as good a shape as possible."

Salazar's tendency to downplay his opposition is unsettling. With the depth of talent on the roads today, with the myriad things that can go wrong during two hours of flat-out footracing, it is surprising that Salazar continues to develop his strategy as if there were no serious challengers in the New York City Marathon field.

A more typical distance runner would at least pay lip service to his opponents, hedging his own bets by complimenting the prowess of a half-dozen other runners in the field and recounting his own weaknesses. Salazar, though, is not typical. He has entered three marathons and won them all. He has predicted a world record and run true to his word. He has climbed out on a limb and stood there, unabashed, insisting that he won't fall. And he has climbed back unscathed.

This kind of behavior earns considerable respect among the public, but deep down it also awakens a peculiar sentiment. Even as they stand in admiration, people begin to yearn for a challenger, hoping that someone will cut the limb or that it will simply break. Life is not predictable, and the marathon even less so. A man should not be so sure of victory, should he?

When asked what strategy he would use if he were Beardsley, Salazar pauses and says, "Not run."

He laughs and adds, "No, I'm just kidding," knowing the furor that some of his past remarks have caused, and seeming to genuinely want to avoid antagonizing Beardsley. Still, he insists on giving the answer he feels is accurate.

"It's just that I really don't think he's as good a runner as me. I don't think he's prepared to beat me. That doesn't mean he can't beat me. Obviously at Boston he was only two seconds away. Anything can happen. But given that I'm running normally and he's running normally, I know that I'm better than he is, and I feel I'm faster than he is. So I don't really see how he can beat me."

Other opponents in the New York field rate lesser responses. A shrug, a simple word or two.

Salazar's contagious confidence notwithstanding, though, one can't help but wonder whether there might be a surprise or two in store for Alberto. Hot weather, a twisted ankle, a progressive tightening of the muscles and weakening of resolve that so many runners face after twenty miles, or some previously untested yet formidable opponent. Is there anything that might upset his plans?

"The only thing that worries me," he confides finally, "is my tendency to have stomach problems."

It is a small concession to uncertainty, but an important one. A man who admits the possibility of surprise is a man in touch with reality. That Salazar has accepted the unpredictable shows that his analysis of the marathon is based on fact, not pride. He has thought things through—his own training, his weaknesses, the things that can happen during a twenty-six-mile race—and only then has he dared to predict, simply, proudly, not boastfully, that he plans to win.

The small concession to uncertainty has put me squarely in the Salazar camp. As the interview winds down, we discuss other things—business, friends, fatherhood—and I watch as Salazar's wife Molly works ultrasound treatment on Alberto's foot, massaging the plantar fascia. I find myself hoping the twinges in his arch will not become Salazar's achilles heel. That there will be no surprises, no hitches, no wrenches in the machinery of his performance at New York.

SATURDAY, OCTOBER 23, 1982   *Race Headquarters, New York City*

We are supposed to be enjoying a prerace press luncheon. Instead, the roomful of reporters is hearing poorly translated answers from the U.S.S.R. marathon contingent. Several times I urge myself to pay attention, thinking perhaps there is a surprise for Salazar in their Soviet midst. In reality, though, the only possible surprise in the room would seem to be in the form of Anna Domoratskaya, whose 31:48 10K last summer suggests her long-distance talent and possible threat to Grete Waitz in tomorrow's race.

None of the other principals is at the luncheon. Not Beardsley, not Gomez, not Waitz. Not Salazar.

At the interview in Eugene, Salazar had given his opinion of prerace interviews.

"I remember Henry Rono, when he first came to the States, saying he wouldn't do interviews because they robbed him of energy. I used to laugh at that and think, 'What nonsense. How could just talking about something bother you?' But now I'm starting to feel the way he did. You get tired of talking about it."

So Salazar is hiding somewhere today, storing energy. Since our meeting in Eugene, he has decided not to make a prediction for the race. He will run to win, of course, but there is no talk of a world record.

Throughout the press luncheon and the rest of the day, speculation will center on the likely battle between Beardsley and Salazar, the questionable challenge of first-time marathoner Carlos Lopes of Portugal, the relatively untested marathon talents of Jon Sinclair, and a few other possible threats to Salazar's dominance. Marathon headquarters and the trade show will be their usual high-powered, bizarre collection of snake-oil salesmen, long-distance groupies, and famous cartoon characters of the running scene.

At the end of the question-and-answer session at the press conference, as the table of edibles becomes uncellophaned, Gary Fanelli steps into the food line dressed in black suit, black hat, black tie, and sunglasses, a la Elwood Blues, as is his custom. His appearance startles one of the Russian runners, who moves out of the way to let Fanelli through, eyeing him suspiciously.

Later, Fanelli wonders aloud whether the Blues Brothers have made it to Soviet television yet.

"They have," I tell him, "but censors change a lot of the lines. For example, Elwood is translated as saying, 'We'd be on a mission from God, if there was one.' "

Fanelli smiles slightly, just as our waiter comes by to ask if he'd like his coffee freshened. "No, thanks," he says, his smile gone. "It's already so fresh I've had to slap it twice." The waiter stares at him. "And this cheese here is so sharp it cut the roof of my mouth." The waiter smiles and pours someone else's coffee.

Fanelli is the only marathoner I can recall at that moment who has run the first half of a marathon in 1:03, as Salazar has claimed he's ready to do tomorrow. And with Salazar and most of the rest of the top runners resting, it is up to Fanelli to represent a 1:03 half-marathon runner. Now, he is looking at the waiter through dark glasses, saying, "You know how to whistle, don't you? You just put your lips together and blow. . . ."

SUNDAY, OCTOBER 24, 1982 *Fort Wadsworth*

There is something dangerous-feeling about marathon morning in New York. Whether it's the early-morning scramble to the shuttle buses, or the long ride to the starting line, or the crush of sixteen thousand runners at Fort Wadsworth, huddling in green garbage bags for warmth, or the surge of bodies through the gates near the Verrazano Narrows Bridge, or the chop-chop-chopping of helicopters above, or the pungent aroma of analgesic and sweat, there is something threatening and yet energizing in the air, like aerosol adrenalin. War, or a riot, is afoot.

In the press room at Fort Wadsworth, Mayor Koch walks in, wearing an "I Love NY" scarf. A few people gather around him to shake hands and smile inanely.

Much of the speculation about Salazar has now turned to whether he'll show up wearing his Athletics West jersey and Nike shoes, or whether his agent has sold his chest and feet to someone else. My own feeling is that Alberto will make no major change before the race. If interviews are draining, business is worse, and I can't imagine him risking a marathon victory for any amount of money. To his credit, Salazar has avoided the majority of road races to protect his ability to race well in a few, keeping his sights on long-term goals.

"My goals are of ultimate improvement, and running more races isn't going to help that," he had said in Eugene. "The money isn't really that important."

Important or not, Salazar shows up in his usual gear and begins loosening up with the rest of the runners in the gymnasium.

SUNDAY, OCTOBER 24, 1982   *On the Bus*

As Ken Kesey once said, "You're either on the bus or off the bus." I'm on.

There are eighteen reporters and several dozen donuts on the media wagon. The rig, a Hertz courtesy van, is full, and marathon media guru Joe Goldstein has the unenviable task of refusing admission to anyone who hasn't qualified for this New York City Marathon Holy of Holies. Goldstein has checked my credentials at least four times, and he's thrown maybe twenty people off the bus. He is friendly, nasty as nails, and seemingly wired on adrenaline and caffeine. Goldstein is the perfect Ahab for our media ship.

On another vehicle, a truck with a multitiered platform facing backward, are several dozen photographers. It's not easy getting on that vehicle either, and those guys don't even seem to have donuts and a TV monitor as we do. As it turns out, they won't have any good camera angles either.

The temperature is just shy of fifty degrees, and the wind is uncooperative to the tune of a ten-mile-an-hour head wind. As sixteen thousand people settle into their blocks, there is a kind of stillness, punctuated by helicopter noise overhead. The runners have left behind cheap sweats and garbage bags to be donated to New York's needy, and now they pause, ready to go. An aerial burst says they're off.

Just before the start, there's a TV close-up of Salazar at the starting line. The image strikes me as unusually tense. The normally calm, confident Alberto looks tight and worried. Is there a surprise in store? Has someone gotten under Salazar's skin?

For the next couple of hours, our bus is part of a wailing, careening, gawking, vehicular entourage for the leaders of the New York City Marathon. Our driver, Barbara, follows the blue line across bridges, through crowds, around tight turns, and over potholed New York streets, trying always to satisfy the needs of the writers within. Theoretically, we are to follow the instructions of field general Fred Lebow, relayed from his jeep to the radio operator on board the bus, then communicated to Barbara. In reality, we are in a two-hour battle for viewing supremacy with the photo truck, with twenty reporters barking instructions at once.

"Speed up!" someone shouts.

"Slow down! We can't see!" someone else screams from the back.

"Don't let the photo truck get behind you!" yells Goldstein.

"What's the hurry?"

"Stop, Barbara! Don't go any further!"

"What the hell! We're miles ahead! Slow down!"

"Fred says to keep moving!"

"The cop says to move over!"

"What's wrong with our driver, Joey? Can't she understand English?"

Whatever drugs Barbara might have been on, she handled the constant abuse wonderfully, with only slight lapses into exasperation. With Barbara at the helm, our bus caught momentary glimpses of Salazar and friends whenever we were fortunate enough to outsmart one or two of the other vehicles. Most of the time, though, we all watched TV at the front of the bus.

In spite of the difficulty of our vantage point, it was a genuine kick to be at the front of the pack, watching as best we could as Salazar plummeted along, shadowed by a dwindling pack of contenders. The pace, slowed by the wind, was still under five minutes per mile, as Alberto managed to shave runner after runner from the lead group.

There is indeed a transcendence to sport. As we headed across the Queensboro Bridge, the Manhattan skyline seemed suddenly to leap into view, while helicopter blades whipped the air, sirens wailed, and a small pack of marathon runners headed into the bosom of Manhattan, where thousands upon thousands of spectators stood waiting to welcome them. It was hard to believe there was anything happening anywhere else in the world. There was only this group— Alberto Salazar, Rodolfo Gomez, and a handful of other runners— striving to outrace one another in the streets of New York.

Salazar had passed the half-marathon in 1:04:53, not the furious 1:03 anticipated. Still, there had been few runners left, and by twenty miles only three—Salazar, Gomez, and Lopes—were in contention. Suddenly, Gomez made a break, moving a few strides ahead.

We learned later that a side stitch, the kind of stomach cramp alluded to in Eugene, had been bothering Salazar. Alberto tried to relax without letting Gomez get away, and in fact it was only for a few hundred yards that Gomez had the luxury of a lead. Just as suddenly, Salazar was back running with the Mexican.

The brief but clean break suggested that Gomez might yet pull an upset, that Salazar's side might bring him to his knees. I wondered if Salazar remembered calling Gomez unpredictable in Eugene. I wondered if Rodolfo had him worried.

In truth, it seemed not. As early as twenty-three miles, as the two went head-to-head in Central Park, I was picking Salazar. Though Gomez was tenacious, answering every surge with a countersurge, it seemed that Alberto was calling the shots, defining the race. Later, he would say he felt a need to soften up Gomez with repeated surges, knowing the Mexican's formidable finishing kick.

With a few hundred yards to go, in a cloud of dust and with a hearty heigh-ho silver, Salazar sprinted one final sprint to the finish line, leaving Gomez behind, winning the 1982 New York City Marathon by four seconds. It had been one hell of a race.

SUNDAY, OCTOBER 24, 1982   *Minneapolis*

I have beat a hasty retreat from New York City, running from the postrace press conference to the hotel to the taxi to the airport to the plane. A long flight to Minneapolis has gone by quickly, lost in a stupor of fatigue.

With a layover in Minneapolis, I head out for a run in the dark, soon finding my way to a nearby state park. I run quietly along the dark trails, remembering Salazar's stunning, third-time victory at New York a few hours earlier.

At the postrace conference, an exhausted Dick Beardsley had sat confused, wondering why, on that day of all days, his legs had decided to cramp. In answer to a question about Salazar's seeming dominance of the marathon, Beardsley had said, "No one is unbeatable."

Gomez, looking somewhat fresher than Beardsley, had answered a similar question by saying, "Salazar is a great runner. But I don't think he's invincible."

Invincible or not, it had been Salazar's day. On that Sunday in October, he had beaten the best. There are other runners remaining—De Castella, Seko, a few Ethiopians—but on that day Salazar had proved himself king. He had won what New York City sportswriters were calling "The Duel in the Sun."

As I run in Minneapolis, though, with only the moon for companion, it would seem to be a day for dreams, not dueling. A time to wonder if Salazar—confident, proud—would be able to continue to put together the training needed to remain at the top, to shake off the determined, bold challenges of people like Gomez.

"More and more people seem to be moving from the track into

the marathon," Salazar had said at the press conference. "By 1984, it's going to be tough to win a medal."

Still, running in the dark, with the moon as my witness, it already seems impossible to imagine anyone but Salazar winning any marathon in which Alberto Salazar is a participant.

Fame

SOMETHING ABOUT THE FACE was familiar. Perhaps it was the expression. The eyes of a hunted animal.

I had just boarded a plane in Spokane, headed for Kansas City by way of Denver. I had been busy jockeying my bag under the seat in front, trying to catch an unnoticed glance at the girl sitting next to me and watching other passengers board, when I saw those eyes.

Double-take.

(*"I know I've seen that face somewhere,"/Big Jim was thinking to himself./ "Maybe down in Mexico,/Or a picture upon somebody's shelf."*)

Bob Dylan! Songster, star, semireluctant guru of the rebellious sixties. The rest of his band was boarding the plane too. I turned as discreetly as I could to catch another look, but he had already found his seat. My pulse had picked up.

"Wasn't that Bob Dylan?" I asked the girl to my left, the one I had been peeking at before.

She looked at me. Young, blonde, dull. "I don't know," she said indifferently. "I didn't see him."

Probably into New Wave, I guessed, thus explaining her lack of enthusiasm for Dylan. I tried to stand up to look for the Jester again, thought better of it, and sat down. I vowed to get another look later on.

Fame, as we all know, is a two-edged sword. Fame is a flame. It warms and enlightens. It burns and destroys. It blazes and flickers and is gone.

In 1976, a few months after a surprising, gratifying fourth-place finish at the Montreal Olympic Marathon, I was sharing a taxi ride with the man who was a supposed failure because he had finished second in that same race: Frank Shorter.

Frank had won a race in Charleston the day before, and I had finished way, way behind. As we rode toward the Charleston airport, I in the front seat of the taxi, Frank in the back, the driver noticed Frank's trophy.

"You won yourself some hardware, eh?" he said.

"Yep," Frank answered quietly.

"You musta done pretty well in the race yesterday, eh?" the driver added.

"I guess so," Frank responded.

By this time it was obvious that the driver didn't know who was riding in his cab. I took it upon myself to introduce the two.

"This is Frank Shorter," I told him. "He won the race yesterday."

The driver looked in the rearview mirror. "You're not really Frank Shorter, are you?"

Frank nodded. "Uh-huh."

"Nah, you're not Frank Shorter."

"Hey, really," I said, amused. "He's Frank Shorter, and that's the trophy he won yesterday."

"You're really Frank Shorter, eh?" he said, looking in the mirror again. There was a long pause. "What happened to you at Montreal?"

Frank looked at me, shrugged, and began some sort of explanation.

Back on the plane to Denver, I had pieced together a theory. Dylan had played a concert in Spokane and was now on his way to Denver for another. As a born-again Christian, he had rejected unnecessary vanities like his own plane. He was flying coach with the rest of us normals.

I wanted to discuss my theory. The blonde to my left was obviously out. To my right, across the aisle, an impressive-looking woman was reading a track article in *Sports Illustrated*. Another double-take. *I know I've seen that face somewhere. . . .*

I sat back. I know her too, don't I? Didn't I? I put my hand over my eyes, concentrating.

When I was in the seventh grade, parochially incarcerated, it was difficult for us boys to find a decent role model among the assorted nuns who made up the teaching staff. A nun who would step up to the plate and take a few swings during noontime softball games was an instant hit, so to speak, among us guys, but none of us hoped to grow up to be like her someday. You know what I mean.

One day, though, a miracle occurred. Our principal hired a P.E. instructor who played baseball for the Seattle Rainiers.

We were in heaven. A baseball star in our midst! He had instant rapport and several hundred new fans. We worshipped him. We begged our parents incessantly to take us to a Rainiers game so we could watch our hero play. Imagine: our P.E. instructor up to bat with the best.

Imagine our disappointment in learning that he was not listed in the official baseball program. He was never in the paper, or on TV. When we finally went to watch a game, he was nowhere to be found.

That was his last year as an unheralded third-string Seattle Rainier. That was his only year as our adored P.E. instructor. The disappointment and disillusionment I experienced were the beginning of my understanding of the responsibilities and pitfalls attached to "fame."

Riding to Denver with Bob Dylan, I had just figured out who was across the aisle from me. I leaned over.

"You're Kate Schmidt, aren't you?"

She was. The top-ranked U.S. spear-chucker, fourth-place Olympic Games javelin competitor. We discussed track and field for a while, the impending boycott, and the Athletics Congress, until I finally had to say what was on my mind.

"Did you see Bob Dylan get on the plane?"

Her eyes lit up. "That *was* him. I thought that's who it was."

We talked a little more, but I was agitated. I wanted to look again. I got up from the seat and, pretending I needed to visit the bathroon, I sauntered to the back of the plane. He was nowhere to be seen.

In the bathroom, I stared at myself in the mirror. Where could Dylan have been that I hadn't seen him on my way back? But then again, what difference did it make? I headed back to my seat, still without catching sight of him.

A friend of mine does a great impression of a certain type of customer who comes into my store. In my friend's parody, he comes awkwardly up to the counter, staring in mock admiration, thrusts out his hand, and says, "You're Don Kardong, aren't you? I just wanted to shake your hand. I saw you on TV in the Olympics."

I cringe when he does this. And as I sat flying to Denver, I imagined myself confronting Bob Dylan, trying to come up with an approach that would be genuine and unique. But all I could think of was, "You're Bob Dylan, aren't you? I just wanted to shake your hand. Et cetera."

In Montreal I remember facing hundreds of people I had never met before, but who felt they knew me by virtue of my place on the Olympic team. Generally these were people who wanted to sit watching an event and say, "Hey, I met that guy down there yesterday, and he said . . ." We all know what it's like, right?

I got so used to the hoopla and attention, and all the assorted duties and responsibilities of being the spectatee, that it began to warp my perspective on how people were perceiving me, and even on what I was doing there.

Was I running for their benefit, for the benefit of my country, or for myself? Or what?

By the time I returned to Spokane, the relative importance of the Olympics and my own participation and success there were distorted. I was reminded of this one day when I went to get my hair cut.

The stylist was bemoaning the state of my coiffure, saying in disgust, "Where'd you get this cut last, anyway?"

"In Montreal," I told her, sensing the next question.

"What were you doing there?"

"I was running."

I waited for her to tell me how excited she was to be cutting the hair of an Olympic runner. Instead, after a confused pause, she said, "Running from what?"

My ego shrank. I had learned something about athletic fame.

("*There must be some way out of here,*"/*Said the joker to the thief.*/ "*There's too much confusion.*/*I can't get no relief . . .*")

When we landed in Denver, Kate and I got off the plane and waited. After a minute, Dylan and his band came walking down the gangway. We stared. ("*I just wanted to shake your hand . . .*") We walked ahead.

Halfway down the passageway to the main terminal, Kate and I stopped. A group of Hare Krishnas were campaigning. Or were they Moonies? Certainly they were not born-again Christians, which Dylan and his group were. Kate and I stood by to watch the confrontation of the century, from which lyrical pearls of Dylanesque wisdom were bound to fall.

It didn't happen. The Dylan group eased through the others like a breeze through the branches of a tree. Slight rustling.

Kate and I walked behind them. It had begun to dawn on me that we were acting foolishly, but we continued to follow anyway, keeping our distance.

The group came across a man holding a sign that read, "Krishna Never Died . . . Because He Never Lived!!!" This was a Christian, campaigning to throw the Hare Krishnas out of the airport. There was an exchange between Dylan and the man, then the group went on.

I hurried up to the man. "What did he just say to you?" I asked.

"Oh, he just said that if I needed help getting the Krishnas out of the airport, he and his friends would be willing."

"Do you know who that was?" I asked, hoping to enlighten him.

"No, who was it?"

"That was Bob Dylan." I waited for the amazement to show.

"Who's that?" he finally said.

We walked on into the main terminal. Kate, tired of the game, left to visit some of the shops. I followed Dylan down to the baggage area. As he stood with friends, waiting for bags to arrive, I took a good look at him and decided I was never going to get up the nerve to talk to him. It was time to stop star-gazing. I walked away.

Ten minutes later I was back, wandering slowly by, eating an ice-cream cone. I wanted one more look.

Up until this point I imagined I had been discreet. I had watched without interfering. I had enjoyed proximity to a great star, but I had not bothered him. He did not even know I was there. So I thought.

As I walked by for my last look, Dylan suddenly looked right at me. Stared at me. Glared at me. I looked away.

I headed sheepishly back to the plane, with Dylan's eyes still in my mind. There had been some anger and some pain in them, but mainly they held a desire to tell me something. "I know you've been following me. Leave me alone." The eyes were human, the same hunted eyes that had spoken of the cutting edge of fame when I first saw them, when he first got on the plane. They were eyes that told a lot about fortune. They were eyes that were difficult to look at.

(People called and said,/"Beware, doll, you're bound to fall."/You thought they were all . . . kiddin' you.)

In 1977, Frank Shorter was injured. Having committed himself to run a ten-kilometer road race in Seattle, though, he showed up in spite of the pain. He finished fortieth, having to swallow a lot of athletic pride.

Afterward, a young runner noticed him in the crowd, and went quickly over to him.

"Hey, you're Frank Shorter, aren't you?" The young fan spoke in admiration.

"No," Frank said, with considerable wit and wisdom. "But I used to be."

Peking, Out My Window

IT WAS 1975, my first year of teaching. A year earlier, I had run a personal best of 12:57.6 in the three-mile, following in the slipstream of Steve Prefontaine and Frank Shorter. I had chased Prefontaine in particular for several years, never quite able to beat him but always inspired by his example.

As I remember, when training or racing on a track, I would often discover myself trying to imitate Prefontaine's style, his self-assuredness, and even his irritating habit of getting just far enough ahead of the rest of the pack to be able to cock his head slightly to the left around each turn, keeping the competition in view, letting them know who was in control. Truly, he led a lot of his competitors to their own best efforts, through inspiration, intimidation, and excellence.

And then in 1975, a year after being pulled along by Prefontaine to a personal record at three miles, and largely on the basis of that performance, I was invited to join a U.S. track and field delegation to the People's Republic of China. I left my classroom behind to take advantage of the unique opportunity.

Gerald Ford was in Washington, and George Bush was in Peking. So were Mao Tse-tung and Chou En-lai, the Oscar and Felix of the Chinese Revolution, though both were teetering on death's edge. Great changes were occurring in China, as evidenced by the invitation to ninety U.S. track and field athletes to tour the country in the spirit of friendly competition.

We entered Red China (we were advised not to call it that) along a narrow footbridge outside Hong Kong and went on to Canton by train. During the next two weeks, we competed three times—in Canton, Shanghai, and Peking—and learned as much as we could about the country. The Chinese were friendly, inquisitive, subdued. They were patient in tolerating the strangeness of their Western

167

guests, though wherever we went we were greeted with intense curiosity. Very few Americans had been in China for nearly thirty years.

Our first impressions were positive. The Chinese had gone a long way toward solving the age-old problems of hunger, disease, and shelter. After two weeks, though, virtually all of us were anxious to get out. For cowboys and cowgirls, this was a land with too many fences.

I recall Gary Tuttle, one of the strongest defenders of China's achievements, jogging around a practice track in Peking on our next-to-last day. Somewhat disillusioned after two weeks, he was yelling at some workers, "In the States you guys would be making eight bucks an hour. How do you like your jobs since Liberation?"

Unaware of what he was saying, they seemed to like them just fine.

Today, almost ten years later, those of us who made the trip still relive those two weeks of unusual travel whenever we get together. These are some of the other memories that have stuck with me, distilled through time, edges blurred. With luck, most of the facts are there. I know the essence is right.

We are on the outskirts of Hong Kong on the train, having stopped at a village to pick up passengers. An old man, perhaps eighty, is pushing a handcart, stacked high with milk bottles, along the loading platform. He is bald, with a stringy beard that hangs from his chin like gray moss.

As he moves his cargo past the train windows, one wheel of the cart hits a rut, and the load falls over. Dozens of milk bottles hit the pavement, spraying glass and milk everywhere.

For a moment the old man stares at the mess. Then, like an actor, he slowly turns to face his audience watching from the train windows. A wonderful smile wrinkles his face.

I can still see his toothless grin. Chinese philosophy could not be better represented.

We are in Canton, where the weather has been warm and humid. I decide to go for a run with Dick Buerkle, a 5000-meter runner who will later set the American record for the mile indoors. In China he is mischievous and irreverent. He has already decided that what the Chinese need is not improved technology or greater political freedom or fewer hassles from the Soviet Union. What they need is eight hundred million joy buzzers.

Buerkle is known for many things. He runs, at least at times, with bells on his feet. Tiny bells like the Hare Krishnas wear, but for Buerkle they hang on his shoelaces like the sun and the moon, establishing a rhythm for his running.

Buerkle has also been known to let out loud grunts during a race. Just his way of forcing trapped air out of the diaphragm. Fellow runners consider the practice unnerving.

Now, Buerkle and I are running through the streets of Canton. People are everywhere—working, walking, transporting goods, selling food, performing various jobs. They scurry antlike in the street, appearing confused but in reality following carefully prescribed plans.

Buerkle and I follow the Pearl River for five miles, then turn for home. Heading down a side street, we pass through a busy market area. As we pass, thousands of Chinese turn to stare.

Is the sight of a tall, skinny American and his short, bald companion, both of whom are running clad only in shorts, so unusual? Judging from the crowd reaction, yes.

We have arrived in Shanghai, which must be the grayest city on earth. The sky is overcast, the buildings are stone, the people dress in drab colors, and the river moves like a lazy rat toward the sea. The only color billows in pink from the top of a chemical-factory smokestack.

During the afternoon, a small group of us have traveled to a meeting with Dr. Chen, who has gained worldwide recognition for his success in reconnecting severed digits and limbs. Fingers, toes, feet, arms, and legs need not fear a premature separation from the bodies to which they belong when Dr. Chen is around. With tremendous skill and microscopic surgery, he has allowed the workers of China to remain the workers of China, machinery notwithstanding.

I am sitting next to a reporter from one of the wire services while the doctor is talking. Dr. Chen describes a case of bone cancer, where an arm has been removed, the cancerous section cut off, and the remaining, shortened arm reunited with its host. He tells of a man whose thumb was smashed by a machine, crushed beyond hope of restoration. In the interest of health and production, though, a big toe had been sewn back on in the thumb's place. And so on.

Someone asks Dr. Chen how such operations are paid for, and the doctor describes a health-care system that includes contributions from the commune and the province, resulting in no expense to the patient.

"That's amazing," I tell the reporter next to me. "In the States, an operation like that would cost someone an arm and a leg."

"Yeah, right," he replies, with no hint of amusement.

We have traveled to a commune outside of Shanghai. On the way, we have passed a virtual parade of vegetable carts, mostly human-powered, transporting produce to the city.

Wherever we go in China, whether to a factory, school, hospital, or whatever, we begin our tour by gathering in a meeting room for a brief preview of what we'll be seeing. The scene is almost always the same. There is an electric fan on the ceiling, and pictures of Marx, Engels, Lenin, and Stalin on one wall. On the other wall, Chairman Mao. We sit at long tables and are offered green tea and cigarettes. The Chinese themselves smoke like greasers, and seem surprised that few in our group do.

In short order, the manager, the headmaster, or in this case the production chief arrives on the scene to tell us how the operation fits into the overall scheme of things in the country, with frequent references to Chairman Mao.

In the case of this particular commune, the man is obviously pleased with its record of production, whereby over two tons of veggies are being shipped to the city daily. This makes his operation one of the most successful in all of China.

"You may have noticed on your trip here," he tells us through an interpreter, "that most of the vegetables are transported to the city by bicycle power. In the future, we hope to switch to a more modern system, with gasoline-powered vehicles."

We all nod politely.

"On the other hand," he says, tongue-in-cheek, "maybe our present system isn't so bad, since we end up promoting the health of the commune through physical exercise."

We chuckle.

"In fact, though," he adds seriously, "there is some truth to this idea, since one of our young men here finished second in the recent provincial cycling championships."

We murmur our approval, while in the back of the room a hand goes up. It belongs to Dick Buerkle, who asks politely, "Does he ride a ten-speed vegetable cart?"

The interpreter struggles to translate.

We have finished a trip to a turbine factory, where we hear of China's plan for increasing production without relying on the fickle support of other countries. China will do it, we are told, through educating the masses to the goals of communism, thereby encouraging diligent work.

Throughout the tour, Dick Buerkle has been irritated by the constant attention to his bald head. The Chinese, whether in an athletic stadium, on the street, or in the factory we have just visited, cannot seem to help staring at this bald foreigner. At the track meet in Canton, Buerkle has confessed to feeling "like a damned monkey in a cage" as he jogs around the track accompanied by incessant murmuring in the stands.

Outside the factory, we reboard the buses, while favorite interpreter Fong Hsu answers our questions about the tour. Buerkle seems intent on being a burr in Fong Hsu's saddle, although he clearly enjoys the man. On another day, Buerkle has let Mr. Fong save him from a contrived tumble into the Pearl River, and it is not uncommon for a tour to be delayed while the interpreter goes searching for the errant Buerkle, who is generally looking for Chinese graffiti on restroom walls. In return for Mr. Fong's concern for his safety, Buerkle has let the man in on the secret of fitting six elephants into a Shanghai automobile ("Three in the front, three in the back"), though Mr. Fong does not understand this example of Western humor.

"There's one thing I don't understand, Fong Hsu," says Buerkle as we sit in the bus outside the factory.

"Yes, what is it?" replies Mr. Fong, eager to educate us on the ways of his country.

"If the Chinese workers are so interested in increasing production and achieving socialist goals," he says, pausing to let the seriousness of his question impress Mr. Fong, "then why do they all seem to have the time to stop and stare at a bald head?"

Laughter reigns, while the irritated Fong Hsu scolds Buerkle for asking questions that do not need asking.

We are at the Great Wall of China. I am *on* the Great Wall of China.

It has taken three buses—two to ride in, one to follow as a spare—to get us to the top of the mountain pass where the wall is, and even then we almost don't make it, as two of the buses break down on the way up.

I try to take a picture of one of the Red Army soldiers, but he waves the camera away. Instead, I focus on the distance, where ruins of the ancient structure zigzag in ribbons across the hills. I look toward the arid regions of Mongolia, where the enemy once gathered to attack, and I look back at the wall, built over generations and generations.

It speaks eloquently of China's historical regard for foreigners.

We are in the stadium in Shanghai. Russ Hodge, our team captain, has asked us to gather, coaches excluded, in the middle of the field before the meet. As we listen, Russ informs us that it has come to his attention that some members of the squad had been smoking marijuana in their hotel rooms the night before, unbelievable as it seems.

"We're here as ambassadors of the U.S.," he says, or words to that effect. "We really don't need to create an international incident. Whatever you do, please get rid of any of that stuff that's around. Enough said."

That evening, I imagine, marijuana that entered China in a pair of socks or a pole-vault pole exits via the Shanghai sewer lines, never to interfere with Sino–U.S. relations.

We are in the main stadium in Peking, a few days before our final meet. During our stay in China, many of us have had difficulty doing long runs. In Canton we had been chased by a taxi driver, motioned to stop, given confusing hand signals, and finally allowed to finish our run. In Shanghai we had been confined at one point to a walled park, later to the stadium, and finally to the courtyard of the hotel where we were staying, none of which had allowed us to run freely.

At other times, though, we had run without restriction through the streets, dodging bicycles and a few automobiles, enjoying the unique opportunity to see the sights of China without a tour guide.

Never had we been told by anyone—Chinese or American— that we could not run when and where we wanted. Our delegation leaders, schooled in the ways of China but blinded by enthusiasm for the place, had insisted during our orientation session that we would be able to run through the streets without objections from our hosts. "Just let them know where you're going so they won't worry," one had said.

But the truth reveals itself abruptly as a small group of us try to leave the stadium to run back to the hotel. The Chinese shut the gates, and the guard motions for us to return to the track.

"Who says we can't leave?" says Buerkle. He repeats this until an interpreter finally arrives. "Take me to the man who won't let us leave," he says. We are directed to our coach, Bob Giegengack.

"Our Chinese hosts don't want you to get hurt," he says. "They don't want you running through the streets."

This is the first we've heard of it, and it irritates me. Do they want us to be safe, or do they want us not to see something? In some sort of absurd ritual, I argue with Giegengack. I ask why the Chinese, if they don't want us running in the streets, haven't told us so. I ask what exactly the problem might be. I ask other stupid questions. Finally, Giegengack clamps down.

"I order you not to run in the streets," he says.

"That's easy for you to say," I reply.

"No it isn't. It's one of the hardest things I've ever had to say."

Fuming, I leave to go sit in the shade under the stadium. Nothing makes a whole lot of sense right now. Not Giegengack, not Chinese inscrutability, not my own overblown anger. The only thing that makes sense is an intense desire to be running freely wherever I choose.

We are in that same Peking stadium, a few days later, during the third and last of the U.S.–People's Republic of China track and field meets. The Chinese have been hopelessly outclassed in this confrontation, just as the U.S. table-tennis crew had been hopelessly outclassed by the Chinese in the first athletic exchange between the two countries a few months earlier.

Now the Chinese athletes, most of whom have been in training for only two or three years, are having to eat humble pie. It must be difficult, I decide, to be embarrassed in front of sixty thousand people. The Chinese, urging "Friendship First—Competition Second," handle it well. Someday, perhaps, they will be a track and field powerhouse.

My race, the five thousand meters, is near the end of the meet. I am expecting no competition from the Chinese, but my mind is on qualifying for the U.S. National Outdoor Championships in a few weeks. The time I need to hit is about 13:20 for three miles. Twelve laps, right?

Gary Tuttle, Ted Castaneda, and I have agreed to share the lead, trading two-lap segments. As it works out, Castaneda is scheduled for laps eleven and twelve, so I trail him into eleven-and-a-half laps and then kick, sprinting wildly to the finish of the twelve laps, crossing first.

Unfortunately, a 5000-meter race is twelve-and-a-half laps. I realize this after pulling up and watching the other runners continue sprinting toward the real finish line. "I was wondering why you were kicking so hard with a half lap to go," Castaneda says later, after I follow him in.

I realize what it's like to be embarrassed in front of sixty thousand Chinese. I also realize how difficult it is for a six-foot three-inch Caucasian to hide in Peking. Several Chinese fans point and grin at me later.

It is the evening after the meet, our last night in China. For a group of American postadolescents, we have behaved ourselves remarkably well until now. But we have been confined a little too long, we have resisted various temptations, and we have been toasting profusely the health of our Chinese hosts all evening, our glasses filled and refilled with a Chinese distillate called mau-tai. The shot-putters call it "high test." Chinese never drink more than a sip at a time, but the Americans are throwing the stuff down with no objections from Mother Respectability.

The Chinese are watching us with what I interpret to be cautious amusement. They have not had a chance to watch Americans at play for almost thirty years, and they are getting an eyeful.

As the noise level increases, a few of the athletes begin to cross the boundary between fun and poor taste. Sino–U.S. relations are perhaps threatened, or so the interpretation goes. Team leader Willie Davenport asks pole vaulter Terry Porter to tone it down. Porter objects profusely, vociferously, and physically, taking a swing at Davenport. Porter is carried out to the team bus, unconscious.

As the party winds down, Coach Giegengack is at the head table, making a speech in praise of Chinese hospitality, the achievements of the current leadership, his hope for future Chinese success in track and field, and/or many other things that a coach is expected to say at such times.

In the back of the room, an unnamed runner is standing on his chair, shot-glass raised, yelling, "Bullshit! Bullshit! Bullshit!" at the top of his lungs, grinning like a Cheshire cat.

We have arrived at U.S. customs in San Francisco, having had two weeks of good fun, a crash course in Chinese affairs, and enough adventures to fuel a storyteller for years. We are tired and anxious to get home.

As I wait to have my bags inspected, Dick Buerkle approaches. One final joke, I assume, although his face suggests otherwise.

"Did you hear?" he asks.

"Hear what?"

"Prefontaine was killed." Pause. "In a car accident."

I have no response. I sense only disbelief and a tightness in my guts.

(SPRING 1985)

Epilogue

As I LOOK BACK to 1975, Steve Prefontaine's death seems to stand as a line of demarcation in my own life. Before then, I was a track runner. Afterward, a marathoner and road racer. Before then, I was a student and a teacher who ran. Later, I became a runner, a race director, a shoe-store owner, an athletic politician, and a writer about running. Running became my work as well as my joy.

The sport of running, so simple and basic, has also changed its character since 1975.

Prefontaine would have been no more likely than the rest of us to predict what would happen to the sport he loved. Running would become unbelievably popular. It would become a profession for the world class. Both of these developments, I think, would have pleased him.

During the same period, though, the Olympic dreams of thousands of atheletes would be disrupted by politicians. This wouldn't have surprised him, but it would have driven him to a frenzy that even fifteen miles at full tilt wouldn't have eased.

A year after Prefontaine's death I finished fourth in his race, the five thousand meters, at the Olympic Trials at his track, Hayward Field, in his town, Eugene. The three spots on the U.S. team were filled by Dick Buerkle, Duncan Macdonald, and Paul Geis. "If those are our three best five-thousand runners," I heard someone say later, "then we're in big trouble." It wasn't true, of course. Macdonald, for example, went on to set the American five-thousand record, and Buerkle became our best indoor miler. But a year after Pre's death, a race without him still seemed inconsequential.

Fortunately for me, I had already qualified for the Olympic team in the marathon, so my fourth-place finish in the five thousand didn't cost me that experience. I was able to witness the Montreal Olympics firsthand, to feel the effect of politics on that event, to find myself representing other people's dreams, to begin to understand what life in a fishbowl is like. One image from Montreal that has always stayed with me is that of a security guard sitting outside the eleventh-floor lodgings of the Israeli Olympic team, machine gun resting on his lap. Inside, I imagine, Olympic idealism kept its head down and stayed away from the windows.

In finishing fourth at the Olympic Marathon that summer, I was instantly transformed from a middle-distance runner to a marathoner. I didn't lose interest in the track, but competitive opportunities seemed to flow more easily from the roads from that point forward.

Prior to the Olympics, I had won the Peachtree Road Race in Atlanta, somewhat mystified at the aura surrounding that event. Three thousand runners! When I returned home to Spokane after the Olympics, I suggested that we try to stage a similar event there, even if we would never have anything on quite the same scale. In 1977, we had over a thousand runners for the first "Lilac Bloomsday Run." Last year, 1984, we had over thirty thousand.

Those who study (if that's the right word) the running boom put its beginning in 1972, when Frank Shorter won the Munich Olympic Marathon. The seeds may have been sown at that time, but before

1976 no one I knew ever mentioned such a thing. After that, though, the boom began to dominate things. Eventually, so many people were jogging on city streets that motorists stopped shouting "Hut, two, three, four!" at them.

With the growth of running in the late seventies, the opportunities for top runners to earn a living from the sport, whether as speakers, consultants, writers, quasi-coaches, or simply as top competitors, grew as well. Unfortunately, the rules governing international athletics didn't allow such unseemly capitalizing on athletic prowess. Absurdly, amateurism stood in the way of earning a paycheck, claiming moral superiority while encouraging runners to cheat to pay the bills.

Prefontaine's spirit couldn't have been far removed when runners finally decided to challenge the rules. At the Cascade Run-Off in Portland, Oregon, in June of 1981, many of the sport's top road racers ran and accepted prize money, in defiance of international amateur regulations. That act led to rule changes at the national and international level that would have amazed Pre, making it possible for many of today's top runners to earn money from the sport without losing competitive opportunities. The existence of an athletes' organization like the Association of Road Racing Athletes would have delighted him.

In 1972, Prefontaine had seen the worst the Olympics had to offer, when terrorists murdered athletes. But afterward, I think, it was still possible to believe that that sort of intrusion was a fluke, a vicious footnote in Olympic history. Today, few people are quite so hopeful, and almost no one speaks with much conviction of the future of the Games. Will they survive? If so, in what form?

Much has changed in the ten years since I last chased Prefontaine, unsuccessfully, around the track. Today I find myself acting as writer, reporter, and interpreter of many of those changes, as well as showing up occasionally as a character in the story. This particular book has been filled with ten years of my attempts to define, enjoy, and reflect on the sport that has changed so dramatically during that time.

And the next ten years will bring . . . ?

I feel certain of only one thing. Ten years from now, I will find myself puffing up a hill somewhere, running a course that I've run many times before. And I will be enjoying myself immensely.